# DIRTY DEFIANCE

BRENDA ROTHERT

CHELLE BLISS

1

## REAGAN

I STRAIN MY WRISTS AGAINST THE TENSION OF THE NYLON rope binding them together. They don't move at all, which is no surprise.

My husband learned how to tie knots in the military, and he learned well. I think the only thing he's more expert in is my body. His large hand is reminding me of that now as he trails it up my inner thigh, leaving a scorching ache in its wake.

"Miss me, Reagan?" His deep voice is raspy with desire.

He knows damn well I missed him, but this is our new game. And damned if it doesn't make me hotter than anything ever has before.

"Yes." It's more of a whimper than a word.

I *don't* whimper. At least, I didn't until I married Jude

Titan. He brings things out of me, though, and he glories in doing it.

"Hmm." He shakes his head and runs his palm back down my thigh, making me whine with disappointment. "I hardly even heard you. You must not have missed me much."

"I did." My eyes widen as I blurt it out. "I missed you so fucking much, Jude. Touch me."

A smile quirks at the corner of his lips. "You want me to touch you?"

"Jude…" Annoyance tinges my voice.

Before he walked in the door a few minutes ago, he'd been gone for nearly three weeks on a work trip. Now that he's running for governor, we don't get as much time for anything anymore. Even sex.

"Taking a tone with me?" He arches a brow with amusement. "I told you to expect this. Remember when you sent me that photo of your fingers in your pussy last week?"

I try not to smile, but it's so hard. He'd told me he was about to walk into a big fundraising dinner meeting over the phone, and I'd sent him the photo as soon as we hung up. He'd sent a growly response about having a hard-on and getting back at me.

And my body had heated in response to those words. Our games are torture for me, but it's a delicious torture I crave.

"I remember," I manage, sucking in a breath as his fingertips graze over my bare rib cage.

He'd told me to be naked when he walked in the door, and I had been—and spread-eagled on our bed to boot. But after letting his dark gaze sweep me up and down as he stepped out of his shoes and took off his tie, he'd told me to get up.

Moving painfully slowly, he'd taken the neatly wound red nylon ropes from a dresser drawer and drawn his gaze up and down me yet again, his charcoal dress pants tented with his erection.

I'd expected a fast, hard fuck. My body had been ready for that. But he'd left me, nipples hard and pussy wet, making me stand facing him in front of a chest of drawers, where he'd made me spread my feet apart so he could bind each of my ankles to a leg of the dark bureau.

And now I stand here, legs open, nipples still hard and pussy still very wet, as he taunts me.

"I'm at a disadvantage, babe," he says in a low tone, unbuttoning the top button of his white dress shirt. His eyes are locked on mine as he slowly moves to the second one. "The other men I travel with can look at the female lobbyists with legs for days. They can spend the night with the women we meet at events who throw themselves at us. But me…" He shakes his head slightly as he reaches the fifth button of his shirt.

I swallow hard, my body practically throbbing with

awareness of him. He's several feet away, but I caught a note of his body wash when he was tying me up, and I can still smell it. My body knows that scent—it means desire so powerful I have no choice but to give in.

The corners of his lips quirk up a little. He knows what he's doing to me right now.

"I can't do any of that," he continues in that low, confident tone I fell in love with when he was my opponent for the Senate seat he now holds. "Because I know I already have the sexiest, smartest, most breathtaking woman waiting for me at home. Other women don't compare. Only you can satisfy me, Reagan. Only my wife."

I lick my lips and strain against the rope on my wrists again, to no avail. My hands are staying bound at the small of my back until Jude decides otherwise.

"That's right," I say, pushing my chest out slightly. "So get over here and let me do it. Untie me so we can fuck."

"Yeah?" His smile slides away, and his eyes darken with hunger. "That does sound good right now. I could just pick you up and slide you up and down on my dick until I come inside that hot little pussy."

My lips part. "Yes. Let's do that." I unconsciously tug at the rope around my wrists.

He tosses his shirt onto our king-sized four-poster bed, reaching for the bottom of his white undershirt and tugging it up and over his head.

Even after five years of marriage, he still makes my

heart race. My gaze wanders across the lines of muscle and dark swirls of ink. That broad, powerful chest is *mine*. Only I get to feel the dips and curves he works so hard for in the weight room. And God, do I want to feel them now.

"Nah." His teasing smile returns. "I'm enjoying this too much."

"Asshole," I mutter.

"What was that?" His hands freeze over his belt buckle.

"I said you're an asshole." I glare at him. "It's been three weeks, Jude. I'm dying here. You told me not to masturbate, and I haven't. But you've probably been jerking it every night."

Jude's expression turns serious. "Not even once, babe. I promised you, and I always keep my promises."

I believe him. He's about to poke a hole through his pants with his hard-on. He just has more patience than I do.

"If I'm an asshole, maybe I should just go catch some news on TV and leave you here to think about things for a bit." He steps close enough to me that I can feel the heat of his big, powerful body.

"No." My whimper is back. "I'm...sorry I called you an asshole."

He steps back and returns his hands to the belt buckle, moving painfully slowly.

"You're the most headstrong woman I've ever known."

The belt buckle clanks as he unfastens it. "It's one of the things I love most about you. But in here, I make the rules, don't I?"

"Yes." It's not even hard for me to admit it. I am stubborn as hell everywhere else, but in the bedroom, he owns me.

"Good girl." His pants come down, followed by his boxers, and finally I get a look at the rock-hard cock I've been fantasizing about.

"You look hungry, Reagan." He gives me a look of mock confusion. "You want me to go make you a sandwich or something?"

"Fuck you," I mumble.

He grins and sits down on the end of our bed, so we're face-to-face but several feet apart.

"Maybe," he says, wrapping a large palm around his erection. "Or maybe I'll just get myself off while you watch."

His groan is long and deep as he strokes up and down his dick two times. My heart hammers and my core floods with heat as I watch him.

"No. Jude…no."

"I haven't touched it once other than when I took a piss since I left here," he says. "I promised you I'd wait till I got back, and…I'm back, right?"

My chest rises and falls as I breathe hard from the sight

of him touching what's *mine*. Doing what I've been dying to do since the first night he was gone.

"What can I do?" My voice is high and desperate. "I'll do anything, Jude, just please stop. Please."

His smile is almost feral as he takes his hand away and stands up. "That's what I like to hear. Complete compliance from my little tiger."

He knows I hate it when he calls me that, but damned if letting it pass without muttering an objection doesn't turn me on. I'm done playing. I *need* to get off.

"I missed you so much," he says, closing the distance between us and bending to kiss me.

He's slow and tender, his lips and tongue taking their time getting reacquainted with mine. As soon as he pulls away, I moan with disappointment.

"I missed you too."

"I can tell you were a good girl while I was gone." He sets a palm on my inner thigh, and I suck in a breath. "Going to bed with a wet pussy every night because I told you to."

"Yes," I breathe. "I did."

He traces his fingers up my thigh, and when he slides two of them inside me, I let out a cry of relief and pleasure.

"Fuck, baby," he mutters. "Look how wet you are. You need this, don't you?"

"Yes."

He kisses my neck, his lips finding the spot beneath my

ear that drives me wild. Jude is the only man who has ever known my body like this. He catalogues every inch of me, his goal to make every time better than the last. I'm pretty damn lucky he's mine.

I move my hips in time with his fingers, and when his fingertips glide over my clit, I moan with abandon.

I'm so close already. I was on the edge before he even touched me. He pulls his face from my neck and watches my expression as I come so hard I practically scream. Tears are welling in my eyes from the intensity of it as I come down from the high, panting.

"So fucking hot," my husband says, kissing me softly. "I was fantasizing about that the whole flight home. Watching you come like that."

I feel like I could melt into a puddle of sated satisfaction. I return his kiss, and he cups my face in one hand. Then he bends down to untie my ankles from the chest of drawers.

"Want me to make dinner now, love?" I ask.

He turns his intense expression up toward me. "Good one. As soon as these are off, you're bending your ass over that bed. And don't expect me to untie your hands until I'm done with you."

And just like that, my relaxation unravels and I'm completely turned on again. My husband is finally home. And damn, did I miss him.

# 2

# JUDE

"You still haven't told me about your trip," Reagan says before slurping her first sip of coffee.

I continue reading, ignoring Reagan as she stands on the other side of the kitchen island. Even after five years of marriage, talking politics with my wife causes more headaches than anything. The make-up sex afterward is always off the charts, but the days of agony and anger aren't worth the continual strain on our relationship.

When I don't answer right away, she curls her fingers over the top of the newspaper and pushes down. "Hey."

I peer up, taking in her messy hair and mascara smudged under her eyes. She's still as beautiful as the day I first laid eyes on her. "Hey," I say, still trying to avoid anything that's going to spoil the good mood.

She tilts her head, narrows her eyes, and slides her

coffee mug onto the counter. "I'm not asking as your opponent or campaign manager, I'm asking as your wife."

A small smile plays across my lips as I set the newspaper down on the cold granite counter. "You can't separate the two, love."

She leans over the counter, letting my button-down dress shirt fall open and exposing her breasts as she starts to play dirty. "Baby," she says sweetly, trying to manipulate me. "You know that's not true. I just want to know about my *husband's* trip." She strokes her fingers down her chest, letting the tips disappear between her cleavage as my eyes follow. "You weren't very talkative while you were gone. Is there something I should be concerned about?"

I shake my head, eyes locked on her fabulous tits and wonder if I can distract her with my cock instead of my long itinerary. "What would you have to be concerned about?"

She traces the swell of her breasts, taunting me more. "Maybe you were with another woman."

My gaze snaps to hers as anger zips through my veins. "Don't be foolish," I hiss and slide off the stool, stalking around the counter toward her. She turns as soon as I'm behind her and places her hand on my chest as I cage her in. "There's no one else I want more than you, Reagan. Don't play head games with me when I don't want to discuss work."

She curls her fingers until her fingernails bite into my skin. "I'm not playing games, Jude."

I grab Reagan's wrists, peeling her hands away from my chest, but I don't let go. "You know exactly what it's like when you're campaigning. There's no time to even sleep, let alone have an affair. None of this would be an issue if you would've just come along with me as I asked."

She grunts, trying to pull her wrists away from my grip. "You know I can't leave my job. I might not be running for governor, but my work is no less important."

I move her hands around her back, bringing my face closer to hers. "I never said it was, sweetheart."

She twists her lips in anger. She hates when I call her sweetheart. "Jude," she hisses, pushing her chest against mine as she wiggles in my hold. "Let go of me."

"No," I tell her as I slide my lips along her jaw, moving toward her mouth. "You're mine. You're angry for no reason, and I'm not letting you go until we sort this shit out."

"I…" She doesn't get another word out before I cover her mouth with mine, sealing whatever she was going to say inside. Her body sways forward, melting into me as my tongue sweeps inside and tangles with hers.

Reagan presses her breasts against my chest and rubs her thigh against my dick as she moans. My dick hardens, even though I know she's playing a game, I can't stop my reaction. Three weeks away from Reagan was almost unbearable, and just when I was about to hit my breaking point, I came home.

She whimpers as my mouth leaves her and drifts to her throat, licking the softness where her rapid pulse beats underneath. I release her hands, setting my palms on her hips and tightening my hold. Hunger builds inside me, gnawing at my insides as everything around us seems to disappear. I'm consumed with my wife…with the feel of her body, the smell of her skin, her ragged breathing as I grind my cock against her.

I think the issue's dropped because she's just as lost in the moment as I am. Her hands roam my body, groping my ass roughly through my pants. "What are you hiding?" she says with her head tipped back right as I'm about to lick the top of her breasts.

I pull back, moving my mouth away from her skin, and peer down at Reagan. "You have five minutes to ask me questions, and then we're done talking about my trip." I growl the words as the anger that had started to dissipate returns full force.

She licks her lips, and the corner of her mouth turns upward. "Okay, well…"

I close my eyes, holding back a growl because she always does this shit to me. "Time's tickin'."

"Who did you meet with yesterday? It wasn't on your itinerary, and I couldn't reach you when I called."

"That's what this is all about?" I raise an eyebrow, still

stalling because she's asking about the one person I don't want to discuss with her.

"Yes." She raises her chin.

I rub the tension out of the back of my neck, and my raging hard-on disappears because the battle hasn't even begun. I know as soon as I say his name, she's going to go from agitated to pissed off in a heartbeat. There's no reason to keep stalling. Reagan will find out one way or another once my campaign donors become public. Dragging things out will only make the end result that much worse. "I met with Dominic Marino," I say, ripping off the Band-Aid quickly and readying myself for the blowback.

She's quiet for a moment. Her eyes widen as she stares at me, nostrils flaring as her breathing speeds up when the name I just spat soaks in. "You didn't," she whispers before stepping away from me and shaking her head. "Of all the dumb shit you've done…"

My head jerks back at her words. "Dumb shit?" I rarely do dumb shit. Maybe when I was younger and didn't have so much at stake, I'd dip my toe across the line, looking for trouble. I'm not that guy anymore. As a United States Senator, I can't risk my entire career or my name on dumb shit, as my lovely wife likes to call my actions.

"He's the one person I told you to steer clear of, Jude. What the fuck were you thinking?"

I lean against the counter, crossing my arms over my chest as she starts to pace like a caged animal. Keeping my mouth shut, I watch as her arms flail about and she mutters to herself something about me being a fucking idiot, but I let her words slide.

She spins around on her heels, straightening her arms at her sides. "Say something," she grinds out with her jaw clenched so tightly only her lips move.

I stay still, careful not to make any sudden movements because the wild look in her eyes hasn't disappeared. "I didn't schedule the dinner, but I had to at least make an appearance."

"You should've declined. How many times did I tell you…"

I lift my hand, stopping her from continuing that sentence because there are a few things we need to get straight. "First, I'm your husband, not your employee."

She blinks rapidly, and her eyes widen even more, but I start talking before she can.

"Although I love your input, I do not and will not do as I'm told when it comes to my career." I shake my head as she opens her mouth. "I let you say your piece about Mr. Marino, but beyond that, it's my call on whether or not I allow him to contribute to my campaign. When I'm home, I'm home. I don't want our life to become about work or the campaign. Can you understand all I wanted to do was spend time with my wife and feel like a normal person again?"

Somehow. I remain calm, not raising my voice for a

single word even though I'm so aggravated with my wife and her constant meddling in my career. She treats me like a child, pulling out her daddy card and always explaining to me as if I don't understand how the seedy part of Chicago politics works.

Reagan drops her head and lets out a shaky breath. "I do understand, Jude." She pauses, and I'm hopeful for a moment that the conversation is over. But again, I'm wrong. She raises her head, lifting her chin high, and crosses her arms to match my posture. "But sometimes you need to remember while you were out fighting in a war, I was sitting in my father's office listening to him cut deals with mobsters."

"I wasn't born yesterday." I run my fingers through my hair and try to keep my voice even. The last thing I want to do is ruin the rest of the time I have left before I have to go back on the road again. "I've been in politics long enough to know that if I take his money, I'll owe him a favor."

"You can't," she says and takes a step toward me, completely ignoring everything I just said.

I push off the counter and turn my back to her. I can't fight with her anymore about this. I can't jeopardize the entire weekend over something as silly as a single meeting. "I'm done talking about this, Reagan."

"Where are you going?" she asks as I grab my keys from the hook near the door.

"Out," I grunt with my back to her and my hand on the doorknob.

"Wait!"

I hear her footsteps on the tile as the bottom of my shoes touch the landing, but I don't stop.

I can't.

*Fuck.* I won't.

I love the woman. Hell, I'd lay down my life for hers. I've never been crazier about another human being, but lately, we're like gasoline and fire. The stress of the campaign and the added pressure Reagan continues to put on our marriage by only focusing on my career is weighing me down and killing the dream we gave so much to try to build.

I stalk down the street, wandering to God knows where. I walk for hours, winding down endless streets in downtown Chicago and ignoring every phone call until I end up at the steps of my old gym.

When I walk through the door, my old trainer yells, "Jude! What the fuck, man?" and jogs toward me with his hand outstretched. For a moment, I feel normal again. It's almost like I'm the Marine who just returned from a battle to a warm reception and a kind handshake.

"So good to see you, Manny." My smile's easy as I shake his hand. "Can you fit me in?"

"Can I fit the future governor of Illinois in?" He looks

at me like I'm crazy. "Don't be a dick, dude. We always got time for you."

"I need a few rounds in the ring. No holds barred."

His eyes widen as his hand falls away from mine. "I don't think…" he says, smashing his hands together in front of him as he glances behind his back. "I don't think that's a good idea."

"I can go somewhere else," I tell him with a shrug.

Manny peers up at me with a wicked smile. "No. No. I'll just go easy on you. I can't have that pretty face all messed up for the cameras." He jabs me playfully in the ribs.

I laugh at his statement. "I'll try not to beat you too badly, old man."

He straightens at the put-down and puffs out his muscles, trying to make himself look bigger and badder than usual. "Those are fighting words, Titan."

"Bring it," I tell him.

3

# REAGAN

I don't pay much attention to what I'm throwing into my suitcase as I pack. Some of the clothes are still in their dry-cleaning bags. I'll manage a few work outfits out of all this stuff.

I'm pretty pissed. After three weeks apart, Jude took off on me and won't answer my calls or texts. I missed him like crazy, playing the role of doting politician's wife while he campaigned.

He knows how much I was dreading that fucking interview and photo shoot for a magazine spread about our home life. Even with the cleaning and decorating help his staff hired, I had to make sure everything was just perfect myself. When a photographer is coming into your home, you have to make sure every last thing is on point.

But I gladly did all of it for him. He's only home for

two days before he hits the campaign trail again, and I'm livid that he fucked me and hardly said two words to me before storming out of here.

We agreed before we got married that nothing would ever come between us. Not politics, not my father—our marriage comes first.

But today his fucking ego came first, and I'm not waiting around until he decides to come home.

I've been sidelining my work for months now, focusing on helping Jude instead. And that's been hard for me, because I'm passionate about my work. I'm the US Congress liaison for the Lancet Foundation, an organization founded two years ago to advocate for bipartisanship.

Jude and I have become the poster children for crossing party lines to find common ground. As congressional opponents, we should have been enemies. For a while, we kind of were. But I quickly fell for him, seeing that what brought us together was more important than what we disagreed about.

I didn't drop out of the race because of our relationship, but rather because the revelation about my father's secret family made me reevaluate what was really important to me. But I've taken lots of hits from women's groups within the Democratic Party for stepping aside for my man.

Fuck them. They don't know me, and they don't know us.

I add a couple pairs of heels and my travel makeup bag to the suitcase, zipping it closed. When I pick up my phone, I see a text from Julia, my assistant. She's booked my flight and arranged for me to be picked up in DC when I arrive late this afternoon.

I've been pushing this trip back for weeks, prioritizing Jude and his campaign. No more.

After texting Julia back, I send a message to my husband. **Going to DC for work.**

My anger starts to subside on the cab ride to the airport. Jude was right for thinking Dominic Marino would cause a blowup between us, but that doesn't make him right for not telling me about it.

Dominic Marino buys politicians, plain and simple. He doesn't care what party they are—I've seen people from both sides get in deep with him. He lures them in with his deep pockets and pretense of no-strings friendship, wining and dining them hard. But eventually, he calls in favors, and they're never legal. He stands for everything Jude and I despise about politics.

"Where you headin'?" my cab driver asks, brows arched as he looks at me in the rearview mirror.

"The airport," I remind him.

"Naw, I mean, once you get there. Where you flyin' off to?"

"DC."

He scoffs as he cuts off the car next to us without even

glancing in his mirror. "What's a pretty thing like you goin' to that hellhole for?"

"Work."

The edge in my tone silences him. I'm in no mood to be called a *pretty thing*. No one who knows who I am—or rather, who my husband is—would dare to say such a thing. Jude is charismatic and diplomatic, but he also lets it be known that his wife is hands—and eyes—off.

I've always loved that feeling, that he and I belong to each other. He's careful not to be alone with young female staffers, not just because it can create trouble, but because he wants me to know no one's even *trying* to get with him and being turned down.

The cab driver glides to a stop, unloads my luggage, pockets his tip, and heads away. I'm walking into the airport, suitcase in tow, when my phone buzzes with a text. When I see my husband's name on the screen, I glare at it.

**Jude: WTF? You're not scheduled to go anywhere.**

I want to ignore him, like he's been ignoring my texts, but I'm no good at that. I *always* want to respond. I sit down on a bench inside O'Hare and start to text back and forth with Jude.

**Me: My schedule changed. And btw, you need to be home for the grocery delivery tomorrow at 10.**

**Jude: I'm leaving day after tomorrow for 2 weeks. This is how you want to leave things? Really fucking nice, Reagan.**

**Me: YOU LEFT THINGS THIS WAY, NOT ME.** I'm not some doting wife who will just sit at home and wait for you.

Jude: I'd never mistake you for doting, sweetheart.

Me: Fuck you.

Jude: I'm under a lot of pressure right now. I'd think you of all people would understand.

Me: Shove that guilt trip up your ass, Jude. You shouldn't have walked out on me.

Jude: For fuck's sake…I didn't walk out on you. Stop being so melodramatic.

Me: Stop being such an asshole.

Jude: Come back home.

Me: I'm going to DC for work.

Jude: Reschedule it. I need you with me.

Me: Says the guy who walked out and ignored all my calls and texts.

Jude: JFC, Reagan, I needed to blow off steam.

Me: Well, so do I. You don't seem to get that I'm sacrificing for this campaign. I'm sidelining my work, having fundraising meetings and helping your dumb-ass communications girl every fucking day.

Jude: Of course I get it, but this is for us. We're in everything together.

Me: Bullshit. You hopped in bed with Dominic Marino, knowing it would piss me off.

**Jude: I'm not giving you my balls to keep in your fucking purse, Reagan. You know who you married.**

**Me: This is exactly why I'm not ready for a baby. You pawn off a bad decision by saying it's just who you are, and you run away when things get hard. When I need you most.**

**Jude: I didn't fucking run away, stop saying that. I just needed a break. We talked about trying for kids three years into the marriage, and now it's five years and you still aren't ready. You always have an excuse.**

**Me: My career is not an excuse, you prick. When we decided that, you weren't planning to run for fucking governor. I'm so tired of you thinking I can just find a way to balance everything all the time. I don't have a full staff like you do. It wouldn't be fair to bring a baby into this chaotic life.**

**Jude: Can we not do this over text? Come home.**

**Me: I have to go check in for my flight.**

**Jude: When are you coming back?**

**Me: Does it matter? You'll be gone anyway.**

I POWER down my phone and put it in my purse, standing up to head for the check-in counter. I'm so angry with Jude right now, but I'm also hurt.

Mostly hurt, actually. I miss him so much when he's

gone, and then he pisses away hours of our time together brooding.

I knew who I was marrying—he's domineering, cocky, and strong. He's also the hardest-working, most honorable man I've ever known.

But lately, I find myself wondering if he really knew who he was marrying. He's a smart man, so he probably did know. But did he think he could change me? Tame the one woman who wasn't intimidated by him?

We both communicate with people for a living, so why is it so hard for us to communicate with each other lately? Everything seems to devolve into a fight. The only place we completely mesh is in the bedroom, where Jude's controlling nature works for both of us.

Our bedroom is where I planned to spend most of today, making up for all the sex we've missed out on in the past three weeks. Instead, I'll be sitting at O'Hare for the next two hours and staying in a hotel tonight, away from my husband.

I'm not sorry, though. He needs a dose of his own medicine.

4

# JUDE

"Wʜᴀᴛ ᴛʜᴇ ʜᴇʟʟ ᴀʀᴇ ʏᴏᴜ ᴅᴏɪɴɢ ᴜᴘ sᴏ ᴇᴀʀʟʏ?" ᴍʏ campaign manager Tyson asks as I climb onto the campaign bus and collapse in the booth. "We're not pulling out for a few more hours."

I stare at him across the table, tapping my fingers against the Formica as I grit my teeth. I'm still reeling from the fact that Reagan took off, leaving for Washington without talking to me about it first. I had a few days to spend at home, naked and curled up with my wife in bed, but she went off half-cocked without thinking.

"So, I take it your time off wasn't good," he says when I don't answer his question.

"I don't want to talk about it," I tell him as I turn my face toward the window and stare into the parking lot as the sun starts to rise above the distant trees.

"You better get your house in order."

My eyes snap to his and narrow as my jaw ticks. "My house has nothing to do with my campaign."

He leans back, sliding his arm across the back of the booth. "It has everything to do with this campaign. Your entire platform is family values, and if your marriage collapses, so does your chance to win the governor's mansion."

"We're fine, Tyson." At least, I think we are. Married people fight all the time. Reagan and I are not different from anybody else, but somehow, we're held to a higher standard, which is completely ridiculous.

I go back to looking out the window as Tyson shuffles the stack of papers in front of him. I'm grumpy, on edge, and in no mood to hit the road to shake hands and rub elbows with some of the most corrupt people in the state. Tyson keeps staring at me, waiting for me to look at him, but I pretend I don't notice although I can see him out of the corner of my eye. I curl my hand under my chin and close my eyes, wishing I could do the last few days over again.

"We're heading downstate for an NRA rally, followed by a dinner with a Veterans organization."

"Hmm," I mumble, keeping my eyes closed and letting him talk. I'm taking everything in but not really paying attention. I already read over the itinerary for the week and know exactly where I'm going and when, but that doesn't stop him from repeating everything to me.

"Are you listening to me?"

"Mm-hmm."

He sighs but continues on, knowing I'm in no mood to actually form words until it's absolutely necessary. "Tomorrow's not as easy. We're meeting with some voters who are on the fence. You need to be on point and win them over. Luckily for us, you're polling really strong with the female constituents, so I think you have them in the bag. Just make sure you show up with a little more smile and a lot less anger, 'kay?"

I open my eyes and stare at him. Tyson's been a top aide of mine since right after I got elected to the Senate. He's kind of a nerdy, awkward sort, but he's hardworking and loyal. I had no doubt I was choosing the right man when I asked him to manage my campaign. This is the first time he's had such a high-profile role, and we're both learning as we go.

"We'll get a few drinks in you, and you'll calm down." He smiles and pushes his glasses higher onto the bridge of his nose.

My phone vibrates in my pocket, and I reach down, thankful for the distraction from Tyson. Reagan's name flashes across the screen before going black. This is the first time she's messaged me since she boarded her flight to DC. For a moment, I'm hopeful. Maybe she's going to call a cease-fire, and we can put the entire shitty episode behind us. But as I slide my finger across the screen and take in her words, I know she's digging her heels in deep.

**Reagan: Spoke to a DNC friend last night. Stay far away from Marino.**

I drop my phone onto the seat next to me, and Tyson makes a noise in the back of his throat. "What?" I ask, my voice dripping with anger.

"I just sometimes worry about how that girl affects you."

"*That girl* is my wife," I remind him. "The love of my life, actually. You should really watch how you talk about her."

"You should really watch how you treat her, then," he replies and sets his lips in a firm line, staring at me over the rim of his glasses, judging me.

His words don't sit right with me. I played right into his hand on that one, but Tyson seems to know how to get under my skin and my opponents'. I let out a deep growl as I grab my phone and type a quick message to Reagan.

**Me: I'll take your words under advisement.**

Not the most romantic message, but at least I didn't tell her to go fuck herself like she did to me before she got on the flight. I couldn't give her more than that. Her ability to walk away, even if I technically left the house first, wasn't something I could just let go so easily. She knew what the few days' break meant to me, having been on the campaign trail herself, but she didn't care. Everything seemed to be about one-upping the other, no matter the cost.

"I'm going to get some rest in the back." I stand, taking my phone with me in case Reagan has more to say or I feel the need to tell her anything more. I want to call her so badly. Hearing her voice always helps put shit in perspective, but I can't let what happened slide so easy.

"I'll wake you when we hit Springfield. Get some rest. You look like shit, and I need the golden boy in front of the crowd and working the room tonight."

I grumble under my breath as I head to the back of the campaign bus, closing myself away before collapsing on the bed. I never dreaded being on the road as much as I do this time. Being away from Reagan, especially when we're fighting, is hell on earth. I close my eyes and sling my arm over my face, blocking out the faint glow of the sun and pray for enough hours to feel like myself again.

"MR. TITAN, I'd like you to meet my wife," Mr. Carter, a major donor for the Illinois Republican political party, says as he tightens his grip around his wife's waist. "She's been excited to meet the new face of the party."

My smile's soft as I take her hand in mine and brush my lips against her knuckles. "It's a pleasure, ma'am."

She blushes right on cue, staring at me with dreamy

eyes as she stands next to her husband who looks well over twenty years her senior. "The pleasure's all mine," she replies and licks her lips, looking like she wants more than a simple hello.

Mr. Carter pulls her backward, staking his claim on the younger woman as her hand falls away from mine. "I was impressed with your speech earlier at the NRA rally. I think you're just what we need to breathe new life and secure the future of the party for many years to come."

The man's all business, but then, everyone is at these events. The evening is supposed to be about veterans and the issues they face, especially how I can help make their lives better. But politics always gets in the way. He's dressed to the nines in a tuxedo with his hair slicked back, stinking of wealth.

"Thank you, sir." I dip my chin, keeping the fake smile that already has my cheeks aching securely plastered on my face. "We look forward to doing everything possible to help the veterans and the Republican Party in the great state of Illinois."

"Our contribution will be large," Mrs. Carter says, not waiting for her husband to respond to my statement. "Almost obscene." She grins as she rakes her eyes up my body, not trying to hide her desire in front of her husband.

"My wife and I appreciate your support." I throw that in, reminding her I'm a married man, but she's a married woman and that fact hasn't stopped her from undressing me with her eyes.

"Where is Mrs. Titan?" Mr. Carter asks, glancing around the room.

"She's on business in DC," I tell him as I wish Tyson would find his way to me and pull me away from the Carters. Knowing Tyson, he's leaving me be, praying like hell that the amount of the Carters donation will be in the high six figures.

"I don't know how you do it, Titan. Marriage isn't easy, and marrying a liberal has to cause major problems."

"It's not that difficult. We don't discuss politics."

It's a lie, but the words sound good rolling off my tongue. The very foundation of our relationship is built on politics and our down and dirty race so many years ago.

"Smart man," Mr. Carter says as Tyson finally weaves his way through the crowd to come and stand at my side.

"Ah," Tyson says, placing his hand on Mr. Carter's shoulder, deflecting some of the attention away from me. "It's always a pleasure to see you, Fred."

"We were just talking with your man here." Carter eyes me like I'm property.

I tuck my hand into my pocket, rubbing a stone Reagan had given me to keep my anger in check. She said it helped her in tight situations and thought it would be a useful tool for me on the campaign trail this season. Standing in a crowd of veterans, but having to schmooze with the wealthy instead, didn't sit right with me. There was no greater cause, not even a contribution, that meant more to me than my fellow Marines.

"Why don't we get a drink?" Tyson tells him, ticking his head toward the bar.

"That would be grand." Carter smiles, giving me a quick nod before strolling away with Tyson.

For a moment, I think I'm in the clear, but Mrs. Carter doesn't follow. She moves forward, closing the space between us, and touches my arm. "It's a shame your wife couldn't be here."

"It is, ma'am," I say, sliding my arm out from under her hand and dipping my head. "I'm sorry to run off, but I need to prepare for my speech."

"Of course. Of course." She laughs and pushes her long blond hair behind her shoulder. "We'll talk later I'm sure."

Not if I can help it, but I nod in agreement before heading to the other side of the ballroom and away from Mrs. Carter. She's nothing but trouble. I've known too many of her kind not to know that she isn't interested in my political platform. She wants a piece of the man, the power I could potentially wield. She doesn't give a damn about veterans or my agenda; she wants to get in my pants, and I'm having none of that.

Even on our worst day, when I'm so angry with Reagan I want to throw her against the wall and fuck her into compliance, there's no other woman for me. No one else could ever fill her shoes. She may be a pain in my ass at times, but I know I'm not easy either. We work. We're too much alike and yet completely different that we're a perfect match.

I'm sick of being angry with her. I'm tired of fighting. All I want is my wife by my side, my best friend in this fight, having my back like she always has. I type her a quick message before jamming the phone back into my pocket, praying it'll be enough to at least call a truce.

5

———

REAGAN

I sip my water, pretending to pay attention to Andre Walker as he bitches about the House Majority Leader. It's not that I don't get it—the majority leader is a tenacious woman. But her party has the upper hand right now, and she's just wielding the power any good leader would in her position.

And also, nonstop bitching is my pet peeve. It accomplishes nothing.

"Does she not realize she has to build bridges?" Andre's eyes bulge with his question. "I mean, we *can* make her life difficult."

This dinner was supposed to be a chance to discuss the Lancet Foundation's goals for this quarter, but Andre spent the entire two hours talking about old times and mining for information about my father.

I don't talk to my father much these days, and even if I did, I wouldn't tell Andre about it. He's never been a close friend of mine.

"I need to hit the loo." Andre grins at his feigned British accent, picking up his glass to drain the last of the beer in it as he stands. "Be right back."

As soon as he's gone, I exhale deeply, letting my shoulders sag. It's been a very long two hours of trying to get Andre to focus on the reason I wanted to talk to him. I've also got Jude on my mind. I miss him terribly, and I'm starting to wonder why I gave up all my time with him on this rare campaign break just to prove a point.

*Showing your partner you're stubborn doesn't strengthen your marriage,* our marriage counselor, Melissa, has told us both time and again. *It's not about winning a fight. It's about giving and taking to keep the harmony.*

Our harmony lately has sounded a lot like 80's hair bands. I don't want to be a woman who resents my husband's career. I'm exceedingly proud of Jude and everything he's done and will do as governor.

He's fighting a tough battle for governor against a woman who founded a highly successful tech company. She has unlimited resources to put into her campaign. Jude has to earn a victory by hitting the ground running in every last one of Illinois' 102 counties. Many counties, like Cook, have to be visited regularly.

And he's also still serving as senator. Jude is under a lot of stress, and I know in my heart that I made it worse instead of better by leaving.

I take out my wallet, pulling out my company Amex to pay the dinner bill. When I check my phone as I wait, my heart thuds happily at the message I see from Jude.

**Let's work this out, Ray. I'm catching a late fight to DC tonight, and I'll meet you in your room later. Getting the hotel details from Julia.**

My breath catches in my throat as I read the words. He's coming here. Tonight. Jude Titan isn't a man who chases or begs, but he swallowed his pride and decided to come here to set things right.

My lips quirk into a smile as I remember a conversation we had on our wedding night.

*"Let's never go to bed angry with each other, Jude." I was straddling his lap on our hotel bed, looking down into his dark, intense eyes.*

*"We go to bed angry with each other all the time, love. Then we get up the next morning and have makeup sex."*

*"I know, but now that we're married...I think we should try to always work out our problems before going to sleep."*

*He laughed heartily at that. "We'll be up till sunrise some nights if we do that."*

*"That's not true." I poked him in the ribs. "We just have to agree that some things aren't worth fighting over."*

*Jude's expression turned serious. "I fell in love with you because you're a fighter, Ray. You're passionate and strong and tireless. Never change."*

*"I don't plan to. I'm talking about you backing down so we never go to bed pissed at each other."*

*He flipped me onto my back in an instant, leaving me staring up at him breathlessly. "You think your husband is a man who backs down?"*

*"Not really. But maybe, if properly motivated..." I grinned and bit my lip.*

*"Oh, you don't even know, do you?" He arched his brows in question, grinning back at me. "Nothing motivates me like our fights do. You're the only woman I've ever known who can put me in my place."*

*"And don't you forget it."*

*He scoffed. "I put you in your place a lot more often."*

*When I opened my mouth to protest, he silenced me with a long, slow kiss. I savored the feel of his weight on top of me, his hands pinning my wrists to the mattress.*

*When he pulled his lips from mine, he murmured, "I'm never giving up our makeup sex."*

"Ma'am?"

I look up and see our server standing next to the table. He gestures at the Amex in my hand.

"Would you like me to take care of your check?"

"Oh." I shake my head, returning to the now. "Yes, thanks."

I pass him the card. Andre returns to the table just as the server is walking away.

"Oh, hey, I was gonna get that," he says, giving me a look.

Liar. I've had half a dozen lunches or dinners with him, and every time, he goes to the bathroom when it's time for the check to come and then pretends he planned on paying it.

"No, it's my turn." I wave a hand and smile.

Andre returns my smile, probably feeling chivalrous. "So, how's Jude doing? Looks like Tyson's running him ragged." He sits back down across from me.

"They're very busy, but it's good. Jude's got the endurance for campaigning."

"Probably not as much fun as when he ran against you, though." Andre quirks a grin at me.

"But now his former opponent is on his team."

Andre shakes his head. "I still don't know how you guys do it. You must have some *interesting* dinnertime conversations."

"Always. But I can honestly say that being married to Jude has made me a better person. I see things differently now."

"You guys have one side of your bedroom painted red and the other side blue, though, right?" Andre teases.

Our server returns with our check, and I thank him and open the folder to sign.

"Honestly?" I smile at Andre across the table. "Our bedroom is gray and purple. Gray because things are never black or white, and purple because that's what you get when you mix red and blue. Those are our two favorite colors."

Andre cocks his brows in surprise. "Really? That strapping, tattooed, muscled, gun-toting Republican likes purple? I might have to leak this to the papers, Mrs. Titan."

I laugh at the comment from the man who got his start on my father's staff. "Jude's not ashamed. He mentions it at campaign rallies. We're all about bipartisanship and compromise. Team Purple."

Andre stands, extending his hand to me for a handshake. "The Lancet Foundation is lucky to have you. Let me know how my caucus can help this quarter. You know you have our full support."

"Wonderful, thank you."

"Tell your husband I said hello."

"I will."

We head for the restaurant's exit, making small talk as I wait for my Uber. As soon as it pulls up, I say goodbye to Andre and slide into the sedan.

My heart pounds with anticipation. Jude might be in my room right now. Even after all these years, nothing gets me going like the way he looks at me when I walk into a room. His gaze is always dark and loaded with desire. I've never seen him look at any other woman that way.

I shouldn't have left like I did, though I'm not sure I'm ready to admit it. And if I know my husband as well as I think I do, he intends to make me pay for it in my hotel room tonight.

He puts up with my defiance outside the bedroom, though it drives him crazy at times. But when the bedroom door closes, he's in complete control of me.

Though he knows I like it, I'm not sure he knows just *how much*. My stomach is spinning with excitement and anticipation over the thought of his hands on me.

Touching me.

Teasing me.

Owning me.

We never gave up our makeup sex. We just redefined it.

# 6

# JUDE

I SLEEP ON THE PLANE, GETTING A FEW HOURS OF SHUT-EYE before touching down in DC. Tyson had a shit fit when I told him I was leaving for a bit, and he tried to stop me, even though he knew he couldn't. No events on the schedule until tomorrow night, and at the moment, there was nothing more important than my marriage.

Julia, Reagan's assistant, came through. Not only did she give me the name and location of her hotel, she had my name added to the reservation, so I could swipe a key from the front desk. When I opened the door, Reagan wasn't in there, probably busy talking up some politician over dinner, but she knew I'd be waiting.

I make myself comfortable, kicking off my shoes and loosening my tie before stretching out across the bed.

Staring at the door, I wait for what seems like hours, but is only minutes before Reagan walks in.

"Jude," she says, dropping her purse to the floor and walking quickly in my direction.

I slide down, swing my legs over the edge of the bed, and wrap my arms around her waist. "I've missed you," I tell her as I press my face against her stomach and inhale her scent. I slip my hand underneath her shirt, resting my hand on the small of her back as I peer up into her blue eyes. "I'm sorry I left like that."

Reagan tangles her fingers in my hair and smiles down at me. "I'm sorry for everything too. I shouldn't have been so pissed and pushy."

I laugh, shaking my head as my hand slides down her back and cups her ass. "You don't know how not to be pushy. It's in your nature."

She sighs and leans forward, pressing her lips to mine. The kiss is soft and gentler than I expect after everything that's happened in the last forty-eight hours. "I don't want to fight anymore, Jude," she whispers as she stares into my eyes.

I cup her cheek in my hand, peering up at her with my other hand still resting on her ass. "I don't want to fight either, love. I've been greedy with your time, and you need to focus on your work more."

We stay like that, staring at each other without saying another word for a few seconds. The air in the room is thick as I slide the zipper on her skirt down slowly, letting the metal catch on every tooth, building the anticipation. Reagan and I are always explosive in the bedroom. It's the one place we never argue.

She steps out of her skirt as soon as the material hits the carpet. My breath hitches at the sight of my favorite black lace panties, and my cock hardens. "Were you expecting company?" I ask, looping my finger under the edge of the delicate material resting on her hip and raise an eyebrow.

"No." She raises her chin. "I wanted to feel sexy tonight. I needed to feel more like myself to get through this meeting."

"Who was the lucky person?" I'm jealous when I shouldn't be. Whoever she met with didn't see what she had on underneath her clothes, but I still didn't like it.

"Andre."

Every ounce of jealousy or annoyance I have disappears at the mention of his name. He's the last man in the world I have to worry about. Reagan can barely stand his presence, and even on our worse day, he doesn't stand a chance of seeing her panties.

"I don't like it," I say, because no matter what she says, she likes when I'm a little jealous. She likes when I remind her she's mine, proving to her there's no one else in the world who does *it* for me except her.

She steps backward, biting her lip and hiding her small

smile as her fingers work the buttons of her blouse. Her eyes are on me as she pushes open her blouse, shrugging the silk material over her shoulders and fully exposing her breasts. I reach out, needing to touch her, but she steps back and out of my grasp.

"Not yet," she says and shakes her head, playing a game that I don't like nor have the patience for.

I lunge forward, grabbing her around the waist and toss her on the bed, ready to devour my wife for the first time in days. "Stop playing games, baby." I crawl next to her, settling half my weight on top of her as I cup her breast in one hand.

She laughs, knowing exactly what she's doing, but it dies quickly when my thumb toys with her nipple. "Jude," she almost stutters, and her hips rise off the bed.

I brush her hair away from her shoulder and press my lips to her neck, kissing the one spot I know drives her wild. She turns her head, giving me access to every inch of her soft skin. I breathe her in, becoming drunk on her scent and the feel of her flesh against me. She moans as I pinch her nipple between my fingertips through the lace material of her bra.

"Mine," I remind her, speaking the words as I nibble on the curve of her neck before sinking my teeth into her skin just enough to make her quiver.

"Always," she breathes, spreading her legs farther as my hand slides down her stomach.

I cup her pussy in the palm of my hand, holding her core as my lips move to her mouth. "Forever," I reply before crashing my lips down on hers.

I devour her moans, stealing her breath with my kiss. Our tongues tangle, moving together in perfect harmony as my need builds and my cock grows. Keeping our mouths fused together, I climb between her legs and work the zipper of my pants. There's nothing gentle or sweet about what I want to do to Reagan. I need to be inside her. Deep inside her. I need to feel every inch of her body which I know is mine.

Once my pants are down, I thrust my hard cock inside her, driving her body up the bed with the force. She clutches my biceps, hanging on as I pound into her. Over and over again, panting and moaning as I fuck her like I've never fucked her before. This isn't about love. Only need consumes me and drives me forward.

She bows her back off the bed, pushing her breasts closer to my face. Sealing my lips around her nipple, I rock into her as my orgasm builds. She quakes beneath me, gasping for air. Every ounce of anger and frustration pours out of me, lessening with each stroke until the orgasm crashes over me.

She shudders beneath me, spiraling down the same path of ecstasy and clawing at my skin. I collapse on top of her, resting my forehead on hers. "I love you," I tell her, gasping for air. "More than life itself."

She pulls my face down, cupping my cheeks in her hands and steals what breath I have left with a kiss.

---

We spent the entire morning in bed. Something we haven't done in months. We needed time to recharge, and the only way to do that was shutting out the world. We turned off our phones, unplugged the television, and took the hotel phone off the hook. No one and nothing is going to disturb our limited time together.

Reagan grabs me around the waist and pulls me back in the bed. She kisses the spot between my shoulder blades and rests her hands on my stomach. "I hate that you have to leave already."

I hang my head, wishing more than anything I could stay longer, but we both know it's not possible. I lay my hand over hers, caressing the soft skin with my thumb. "Join me," I say before lifting her fingers to my mouth and peppering them with kisses. "When you leave here, come and be on the trail with me."

Reagan rests her head on my back and sighs. "I don't know, Jude. I'm not sure how healthy that would be for your campaign or our marriage."

"Think about it. I want you with me when you can be." Turning in her arms, I kiss her softly, staring at her as I do. "I always want you at my side," I say as I pull away.

"Tyson would have a fit." She laughs.

I climb to my feet and stare down at my naked wife as she sits with her legs tucked under her. "He could use a little excitement. I don't need an answer now, Reagan, but I want you to know I want you with me."

"Always," she says with a smile before pushing herself up to come face-to-face with me. "Let me wrap up my business here, and maybe I'll find you tomorrow."

Walking away from her gets a little bit harder each time, but I tell myself it's for the best. We both agree that, in the end, the time apart will be worth it to secure the governor's mansion. But right now, with the toll it's taking on our marriage, I hope I win and it's not all for nothing.

Losing at this point isn't an option.

7

# REAGAN

The next day is packed with impromptu meetings, and I don't get a chance to send Jude a text longer than a few words until right before dinner.

**Me: Sorry, babe. Crazy day. Getting a lot done, though. And I somehow landed a lunch with Andrea Matisse! Love you.**

Andrea Matisse is a billionaire philanthropist who rarely takes meetings with lobbyists or politicians. She donates generously to the causes she believes in, but it's well-known she doesn't like being asked for money. I'll have to tread carefully with her so she doesn't think I'm fishing for a contribution for my husband.

I almost didn't even try to get a meeting with her since no one is ever successful, and I knew it would be a waste of time. But then Jude reminded me that the only way to guarantee I never meet her is to not even ask. And now that I get to meet her in a few days, it's not her money I'm interested in. I just have a thousand questions I'm burning to ask her about life, love, and how she juggles it all.

Andrea and her husband Olivier are famously polar opposite. He's a French investment banker from a wealthy family, and she's a shrewd, self-made fashion magnate. He's laid-back and conservative. She's bold and fearless. I'm especially interested in anything she may have to say about what makes their marriage work so well. It's well known they're deeply in love.

A text back from Jude makes me smile.

**Jude: That's my girl. Proud of you, baby. When's the lunch?**

**Me: Thursday or Friday. Her assistant won't have her travel itinerary finalized until Wednesday.**

**Jude: Damn.**

**Me: What?**

**Jude: I was hoping you'd be here with me by then. I understand, though. You can't miss an opportunity like that.**

**Me: How's your day going?**

**Jude: Good. Going to dinner with some donors in 45 min.**

**Me: Who?**

**Jude: The Branch brothers.**

**Me: Ah, nice. They're a sure thing, love.**

**Jude: Yep. I can just relax and have a few drinks and a good steak. Should be fun. Wish you were coming with, though.**

**Me: I know. Me too.**

**Jude: Talk to your boss yet about being able to work from the road?**

**Me: No, didn't get a chance.**

**Jude: Do it tomorrow if you can. I really want you here with me. We can have a Chicago staffer keep up with everything at the house, so don't worry about that.**

**Me: I'll do my best, babe.**

**Jude: Have to get in the shower. Call me later.**

**Me: When will your dinner be done?**

**Jude: It doesn't matter if it's done. I'll step out to take your call.**

**Me: Okay. I love you.**

**Jude: Love you too.**

I TUCK my phone back into my bag and close the door to my small office so I can get some work done. During the day, people are constantly in and out of here, often sitting down to talk. I like it since I don't get to be in this office much, but it's hard to get much done. I'll use this evening to return emails and make a few phone calls.

Since Jude came to see me, I'm feeling grounded again. When things are off with us, things are off in every other area of my life, too. Before I met him, my foundation came from within myself. But now, our marriage is my emotional foundation. He's so much more than just my lover and partner. Jude is my best friend. The yin to my yang. The first person I want to talk to, whether it's about something good or bad.

I notice a growling in my stomach when the sun starts to set, so I order some vegetable fried rice from a Chinese place that delivers and keep powering through until it arrives.

When I finally get to eat, I curl up in the small armchair in the corner of my office, trying to clear my mind of all the things I still want to get done tonight. This job is unending. There's always another connection to be made, another meeting to set up. I like that, but at times, it overwhelms me.

When my bosses hired me for this job, they told me to work at my own pace. Jude scoffed at that when I told him and said they knew damned well I only have one pace—full speed ahead. But I love a challenge, and I'm passionate about bipartisanship. I'm quite lucky to have fallen into a job that works so well, considering I'm a former Democratic state rep who's married to a Republican senator. I thought the political world might consider me a woman without a country when word hit that Jude and I were together and I was dropping out of the Senate race.

I want to be with Jude on the campaign trail. Not because he's campaigning, but because I always want to be wherever he is. But it'll be near impossible to do my job from the campaign trail.

This job requires in-person contact, and DC is where I have most of my meetings. I occasionally have some in Chicago or New York, but most political back-and-forth happens in the nation's capital. If I'm on the road with Jude, I'd barely have time for a few phone calls and emails every day. That's not the kind of job I want to be doing.

And then there's the truth that's been nagging in the back of my mind all day—how can I claim to be working to create bipartisanship when I'm actively stumping for a Republican candidate, even if he is my husband? His opponent is no fool, and she'll be telling the power players in the Democratic Party that I'm all talk about being middle of the road.

I scoop the last bite of rice from the white box and toss the container into the trash can, returning to my desk. If I had a couch in my office, that's where I'd be sleeping tonight. Instead, I'll probably take an Uber to my hotel around ten, talk to Jude, and then crash before getting up in the morning to do it all over again.

I'm enormously proud of Jude and his campaign for governor. But if I went with him on the campaign trail, I'd be there as his wife. He'd have my emotional support. I could charm crusty old donors and chat up women he's seeking support from. We'd go to bed together every night.

But Jude has a talented staff to help him with his campaign. He wants me there, but he doesn't *need* me. The independent woman in me needs to keep some things for myself, and my career means a lot to me.

He's so domineering that I don't think he'd hear me if I tried to tell him all of this. I don't even know how to say it in a way he'd listen to. Jude is like a tall, looming ocean wave—inescapable and all-consuming. We'd just end up fighting, and I hate that.

So, for now, I'm keeping these thoughts to myself. Jude needs to focus on his work, and I need to focus on mine. He's likely to get so busy he'll forget about asking me to join him on the campaign trail anyway, so why invite trouble?

# 8

# JUDE

Louis Branch stares at me over the rim of his brandy. "While you're an honorable man and possibly the best candidate for governor, we still have concerns."

I dip my head, gripping the armrests of the chair a little tighter. The man has been hung up on Reagan since the moment we sat down. He's mentioned her name at least ten times, bringing her father into the conversation too. I'm beyond annoyed, but somehow, I maintain my cool. Coming from a military background, I know how to stay calm in a sticky situation, but politics is another beast and my wife is completely off-limits. "I understand your concerns, but my private life is just that...private."

Tyson adjusts in his seat, clearing his voice because he doesn't like my tone. The glance he shoots across the table is anything but pleasant. "What Jude's trying to say..."

"I know exactly what I'm trying to say," I interrupt Tyson, waving him off with my hand to silence him. "Politics is something my wife and I don't discuss in the privacy of our home. Just as I don't discuss my wife when it comes to my campaign and political office."

"I see," Thomas Branch says before taking a sip of his brandy, staring at me the same way his brother is. "We both understand separating our business and personal lives, Mr. Titan, but every man at this table knows that women have a way of…what's the word I'm—"

"Playing with our heads until they get their way," Louis finishes the statement and laughs, placing his glass on the table in front of him. "I know my wife always has an opinion." He twists the base of his snifter against the crisp white linen and shakes his head. "And her opinions sometimes affect my decisions."

"My wife is not short on opinions, that I can assure you. But she plays no role in my decisions. We're too opposite of each other to ever allow the political realm to enter our home. She has her work, which she enjoys and keeps her focused on her goals, and I have my work, which I believe is important, and I work my ass off to represent my constituents."

"I'm sure your father-in-law has things to say."

I lean forward and fold my hands together on top of the table. "My father-in-law is a piece of shit. He has no part in my life or my campaign. I married his daughter, not the man."

"How did you convince a woman with such a deep political background and fierce spirit to quit the race?" Louis asked, taking another sip. His eyes don't waver from mine.

I laugh at the absurdity of his statement. "You don't *make* a woman like Reagan do anything, Mr. Branch."

"Maybe she's secretly a Republican," Thomas says.

"I can assure you that's not the case." The statement is so absurd, I can't say anything more.

Louis shoves his hand inside his suit jacket, retrieving his checkbook. "Mr. Titan," he says, twisting the top of his pen, "I feel you're a man of your word. I've never heard anything to contradict my perception of you. Over the last five years, you've never swayed from your original plat-form and have remained true to your constituents."

Tyson smirks as he watches Louis Branch write out the check. He's practically salivating at all the zeros. I, on the other hand, am wondering if they're just a more reputable version of Mr. Marino, hiding behind their fancy suits and corporations. Behind that much wealth, there's always a dark side. No one becomes as powerful as the Branch brothers without bending a few rules and strong-arming a few people, including politicians.

Mr. Branch tears off the check, and he slides the tiny

slip of paper across the table but doesn't lift his fingers. "We have faith in you. Don't let us down."

There's a seriousness to his tone I haven't heard before. Every dollar I take toward my campaign feels like I'm digging a hole filled with favors and IOUs. I thought my race for Senate was a pain in the ass, but it doesn't hold a candle to running for governor.

"I will stay true to my platform and the promises I make to the voters."

He stares at me for a moment, probably wondering if that means I'd bow to his wishes when he finally decides to put pressure on me about some issue that could affect Branch Enterprises. But what he doesn't know is his donation is just that and nothing more. It's not a promise for a future favor or passing legislation that'll hurt the people I serve while making him richer.

He taps the check with his fingernail before finally pulling his hand away. I don't move right away, never wanting to seem too eager to take money from anyone because that's the way I'm built.

But Tyson, he's nothing like me, and he snatches the check off the table, folding it neatly before stowing it away in his jacket pocket. "Thank you." Tyson's smile widens. "We'll put this to good use."

Pushing back from the table, I shake Louis's and Thomas's hands before I make up some bullshit to excuse myself from the final small talk. The last thing I want is to sit there and listen to the three of them talk about Washington and "old times."

I walk into my room, shrugging off my suit jacket and loosening my tie. More than anything, including sitting with the three men downstairs, I want to see my wife's face. I fire up the laptop, making myself comfortable on the bed while I wait for her to answer my online call.

After three short rings, her beautiful face fills my screen. "Hey, handsome," she says, leaning forward and pushing the laptop across the bed to get comfortable.

My gaze dips to her breasts as they practically spill out of her top. "Hey, beautiful. I've missed you."

"I miss you too." She frowns as her eyes drop to the mattress for a moment. "How did your meeting go with the Branch brothers?"

Leaning backward, I pull the laptop across my legs and ease back into the pillows. "The same shit as always. They think I'm in their back pocket." Reagan watches me as I remove my tie, her eyes following my hands carefully.

"We both know that's never going to happen. Not with the Branch brothers, at least."

I know where she's going. Or, at least, where she could go after that statement. Probably some small little *innocent* jab about Dominic Marino. "Enough about work. Show me your magnificent tits." I give her a quick wink, being playful but dead fucking serious.

Reagan smirks, lifting herself on her elbows just

enough that I can see down her shirt. "Oh, you're in a classy mood. You mean these?" she asks, jiggling her breasts right into the camera.

"I'm too horny for classy, baby. Come on. Just a small peek."

The camera dips as she sits upright, crossing her legs in front of her body. "This is like old times," she says as she fumbles with the buttons on her blouse, moving so slowly I swear she's trying to torture me.

"I remember you being faster than this," I tease her as I place the laptop between my legs.

She smiles as she spreads open just enough of her shirt to show me the swells of her breasts, but not enough. "If I'm showing you mine, you have to show me yours too. It's only fair." She quirks an eyebrow.

I laugh softly, shaking my head as I pull off my dress shirt and throw it to the floor. I have no problem showing Reagan everything I have, but she's going to do the same. The distance is becoming unbearable, and we've only been apart a few days. The only thing I want is to sink between my wife's legs and listen to her moan my name. I don't want to be alone in an overpriced hotel room. I miss the days of her being in the next room and finding reasons and ways to see her.

"Happy now?" I ask, moving farther away from the camera to give her a better view.

"Pants too," she says, almost giggling.

"Do the same," I tell her, and I'm almost giddy. I remember the last time we had virtual sex over the internet, and it was hot as fucking hell.

I'm all in, totally excited about the entire thing and yanking down my pants like a pubescent virgin teenager with a raging hard-on. She scrambles off the bed, away from the camera, but I can hear the rustling of her clothes.

I practically dive back onto the bed and immediately wrap my hand around my cock, ready to put on a show for my wife. She has a fascination with watching me masturbate. Something I taunt her with often. But she doesn't know I have the same fascination; watching her touch herself is unlike anything in the world.

Reagan slides across the mattress, resting her head on her elbow as she watches me. I could give a fuck what she's looking at as I zero in on her luscious breasts, wishing I could touch them.

"Baby, lemme see your pussy," I tell her, tightening my grip around my shaft, pretending my palm is her beautiful cunt.

"Jude," Tyson calls, knocking on my hotel room door.

"Fuck," I hiss and tip my head back, praying he'll just go away.

Reagan smiles and bites her lip, clearly hearing Tyson's voice and the repeated tap on the door.

"I can see your light on through the peephole, asshole. Open up."

My hard-on instantly dies in my palm. Not even the little peep show my wife's giving me, fucking with my head as she does, can maintain my rock-hard cock.

"You'd better go," she says, spreading her legs open just to make the entire situation worse. "I'm gonna finish what we started. You have fun with Tyson."

I growl and reach for the laptop, trying to get a better look before the screen goes black.

"I fucking hate Tyson," I mutter as I climb off the bed, knowing that what started out as a great end to my evening has died… right there with my cock.

9

REAGAN

ANDREA MATISSE IS NOT WHAT I EXPECTED. OUR LUNCH at a small café has lasted nearly two hours, and I'm not ready for it to end, even though I have another meeting soon.

With her platinum blond hair that falls just past her ears, brown-framed glasses, black linen pants and a pretty dark green blouse, I can see why she is so successful in fashion. Andrea doesn't look like everyone else. She has her own style and no concern for whether anyone else approves of it. Even the wrinkles at the corners of her fifty-something eyes seem fashion-forward.

"Part of me misses talking about fashion every day at a microscopic level," she confesses. "Not just the trends, but the whys behind them. I'd spend hours in meetings about jewelry or hats, listening to my editors pitching articles about fresh ways to cover them."

She shrugs. "But now, I never have to do anything I don't want to do. As a magazine publisher, I had to sit through lots of meetings that weren't my cup of tea."

"Meetings are my life when I'm here," I say.

"And most of them must be with blowhard politicians who like nothing more than the sound of their own voice."

She wrinkles her nose with distaste, and I laugh.

"There's definitely some of that," I admit.

"So, do you talk to your husband about your work?"

"Some. We both try to avoid the things we know will cause a fight."

Andrea arches a brow. "Between a Republican and a Democrat, isn't that *everything*?"

"Not really. Jude and I actually agree on a lot. Too many people in politics focus on what divides us rather than what unites us."

The waiter approaches, and Andrea nods her approval for two more glasses of wine. Fortunately, my next meeting is with my boss, who knows I'm here and will be thrilled the meeting is running late.

"Tell me some of the things you agree on," she says, looking at me over the rim of her glasses.

"Let's see…equality. Jude served with people of all races and backgrounds, and he firmly believes we all deserve the same rights and opportunities."

Andrea is studying me as she says, "Yes, we deserve that, but do we *have* it?"

"No. Not even close. One of the things I miss most about being a state rep was working for the marginalized."

"A privileged white girl like you?"

"Yes. I was raised by a strong mother who came from a poor family. She reminded us often how fortunate we were. We volunteered at homeless shelters growing up, and those experiences really stayed with me."

"Good for you."

I thank the waiter for the glass of wine he sets down and continue. "Jude and I both believe in education. We're for increased funding for public education, preschool, and college. Our country has a lot of bright kids who deserve the same opportunities kids from affluent areas have."

"Agreed." Andrea takes a sip of her wine. "What's something you two disagree on?"

"Ah…we try not to talk about those things." I laugh nervously.

"Worried I'll leak it to the media?" She gives me a shrewd look.

My cheeks warm at the way she read my mind.

"Don't worry, dear. I avoid the media above all others. And you know I keep to myself. Our conversation stays between us. You have my word."

"I trust you." I tuck a loose strand of hair behind my ear and clear my throat. "Gun control is something Jude and I never discuss. And while I may not agree with his views, I do respect them. His military service is part of why he feels the way he does, and as someone who didn't serve, I don't think I get to judge his views."

"Spoken like a true diplomat." Andrea smiles at me across the table.

"I know some politicians double-talk. My father used to say that believing in everything is the same as believing in nothing. I'm not trying to talk my way around anything, I just think that we're never going to get anywhere if we keep belittling others and taking hard-line stances. Compromise is everything. Not just in politics, but in life."

"And when are you running for office again?" Andrea's eyes twinkle as she speaks. "You've got my vote."

"Ah, that's awfully nice, Mrs. Matisse."

"Andrea, remember?"

"Yes—Andrea, I mean. I don't want to hold office again. I realized I'm a much better behind-the-scenes person."

"Behind the scenes for your husband?"

I consider. "Sometimes. But also for causes I believe in."

"Hmm. I feel the same way about what I do."

I can't help a slight laugh. "Andrea, you're anything but behind the scenes. You change people's lives. The money you gave for that clean water initiative in Africa saves lives every day. My work is nothing compared to what you do."

"I wouldn't be so sure. Bipartisanship can create change that will transform lives."

"I hope so."

Andrea takes a silver tube of lipstick from her bag and applies a neutral nude shade. "And do you love your work, Reagan?"

"I do."

"What's one thing you've done at this job that made you feel amazing?"

I furrow my brow as I consider. "Well…I'm still fairly new. I guess, if I'm being completely honest, getting this lunch with you would be my answer."

Andrea laughs at that. "Because I'm the elusive billionaire everyone wants a piece of?"

"No." I smile. "Well, sort of. I mean, there's that. But also because of the work you've done. I read that *Time* article about the scholarship program you created. And when you said the wealthy can waste away their lives on yachts or they can make the world a better place…it resonated with me."

She's giving me that studious look over the rim of her glasses again. "From what I read, you've been on the job for more than a year now. That's not 'fairly new' in my mind."

My cheeks warm. "I guess you're right."

Andrea sits back in her chair, quiet for a few seconds. "And still nothing accomplished that you love, outside of this meeting."

"I love the mission I'm working toward," I clarify. "I believe deeply in it."

"And you'd like a large donation from me."

"Well, I wouldn't turn it down…but no. I just wanted to meet you. Maybe soak up some of your mojo."

She studies me in silence for a few more seconds.

"I'll have my secretary send a check."

"That's truly not necessary, Andrea."

She balks at that. "This from the girl who just told me she wouldn't turn it down?"

I laugh. "I'm not here to play you for money. Can we just end the lunch as two women who know each other now? Who might want to get together again sometime?"

"Certainly. But I'll still send the check. Not because I like you, but because I support the mission of your organization."

"Okay. Thank you for your generosity. We'll put the money to good use."

She glances over at her security men, who are killing time at a nearby table. They rise and come over.

"I do like you, though, Reagan Titan," she says.

"I like you, too. Thank you for taking the time."

"I like you so much that I'd like to offer you a job."

My lips part in shock. "A job? Me?"

She stands up from her seat. "I'd like you to work for me as a proxy, vetting projects and organizations in need of support. I travel in person to check out every cause I donate to for myself, and well…there's only one me. And while I don't believe in lounging away my life on a yacht, I do have a husband who likes to vacation and spend some time with me."

I grin up at her. "You have no idea how much I can identify with that."

"So, what do you say? Will you work for me?"

"I…can't give you an answer yet. I need to talk it over with Jude. But I'm absolutely honored to be asked. Thank you so much."

"I hope you'll say yes. I'll email you some details, and you have my number."

She nods and turns to follow one of the security guys out of the restaurant, the other one trailing behind her and looking from side to side as they exit.

I'm so stunned that I just sit in silence for a minute. The waiter comes to collect the check, and I pay him on autopilot, my mind reeling as I think about the offer Andrea just made me.

After I sign the bill, I take out my phone to text Jude and see I have a text waiting from him.

**Jude: Good luck with lunch, babe. Lemme know how it goes.**

My heart warms with happiness. I looked at Jude's

schedule for today on my phone this morning, and it was packed. He started with breakfast with a veterans group at six a.m. and didn't have any downtime built in until eight tonight.

But still, he remembered my important lunch and texted me about it. That's how he is—stubborn and overbearing, yes, but also the most devoted best friend I've ever known. My biggest supporter.

I need to connect with him for a few days on the campaign trail. I miss his smile, his scent—his unparalleled way of helping me wind down at the end of a busy day.

For now, I have to settle for texting, so I type out a message to him.

**Me: It was amazing. Andrea is so much more than I even expected. She's sending a donation, and guess what??? She offered me a job, baby! I can't believe it.**

I head out of the café to walk back to my office, and Jude responds on the way.

**Jude: A job? Wow, congrats, love. I'm not surprised she picked up on how amazing my wife is. What's the job? What did you say?**

**Me: I want to tell you about it in person. I told her I need time to talk it over with you. Can I join you on the campaign day after tomorrow for a couple days?**

**Jude: Hell yes, you can. You never have to ask,**

babe. Just show up. I'll have my new scheduler get us nicer hotel rooms that night away from Tyson.

Me: Yeah, I'm NOT sharing a room with Tyson. Just you and me.

Jude: Of course. Good thing I packed the ropes.

My stomach flutters in anticipation of being tied up and teased by my husband. I wish I could go to him this second, but I have to stay here through a meeting I have in the morning.

Me: Yes. Good thing. I'm wet just thinking about last time.

Jude: I'm sitting in a meeting with labor reps, don't make me hard.

Me: Me? I would never…

Jude: I'll spank that sass out of you, Mrs. Titan.

Me: And I may come just from that. You won't even need to unzip your pants.

Jude: I'm putting my phone away now. Call u later.

Me: Love you so much, Jude Titan.

Jude: Love u too, babe.

# 10

# JUDE

I SHAKE THE LAST FEW HANDS LEFT IN THE AUDITORIUM. The rally was a resounding success, filling the space to capacity, and having to turn possible voters away because of it.

"Next time, we'll book a bigger venue," Tyson says as he stands at my side as he reviews some paperwork.

"Thank you for coming, ma'am." I smile at the kind old woman as she pats my hand softly.

"My late husband would've loved that a man like you was running for office." There's a hint of sadness on her face as she speaks of him. "He hated politicians but was a staunch supporter of any veteran. He would've been over the moon to see a Marine sitting in the governor's mansion."

"I'll do my best to make it there," I tell her.

"I have faith in you, Mr. Titan. You have the tenacity for the job and will serve our state well." She gives the top of my hand a final pat before she pulls away. "I look forward to watching your victory speech on television."

"Thank you," I say to her before she turns her back and wanders toward the doorway.

"You poll high with the seniors," Tyson says. He's always concerned with the polls and not so much the message.

"Is there a group I'm failing to win over?"

Tyson taps his pen against the papers he's clutching in his hand and twists his lips. "You're split 50/50 with women."

"What? Women seem to love me."

"Liberal women do not, Jude."

"I'll never be able to win over the staunch liberal. That only worked with Reagan." I laugh and shake my head. "But that wasn't an easy victory either."

"You can't sleep with them all, and it's such a shame too."

I cut Tyson a look that says shut the fuck up. "What time is it?"

"A little after seven."

"Shit, Reagan's plane landed. I have to go. She'll be at the hotel soon."

We've only been apart for days, but the time ticked by slowly after the way we left things. Even though we've smoothed over the issues that caused her to hop on a plane and me to storm out of the house, we haven't really solved anything at all.

While she's excited about her new job offer, I have more questions about the toll it'll take on our already stressed personal life.

"Go," Tyson says, but there's no excitement or happiness in his voice. "I'll call you in the morning."

"Not too early," I tell him with a smug smirk. "My wife and I could use a little private time."

He reaches into his pocket and fishes out the key to the new hotel he booked for us to stay in. His taste in hotels this trip has been less than stellar, always trying to control the costs for the long haul of the campaign trail still left ahead.

"Stop being a cheap bastard. I'm sick of shitty hotels. The Branch brothers gave us enough money to at least stay in a hotel where I don't have to sleep on top of the sheets."

He rolls his eyes. "As a former military guy, I thought you could sleep anywhere."

"I can, but that doesn't mean I want to. From now on, make better plans. If we want to win, we can't seem to be broke as fuck because we aren't."

"Yes. Yes. Of course." He waves me off, basically excusing me because he's probably sick of hearing me bitch.

A few nights, I slept on the campaign bus, finding the

accommodations nicer than the shithole he booked for the evening. Tyson was a great campaign manager, but I swear to God, he's become cheaper each year.

I rush out of the auditorium, walking the three city blocks to the hotel. With each passing step, the excitement in my body intensifies.

When I step inside the hotel room, it's empty. There's a message on my phone from Reagan saying her plane took off a little bit late, but she was only running a half hour behind. Just enough time for me shower and get the room ready after a long day of shaking hands and kissing other people's babies.

I pull off my clothes as the hot water from the shower fills the small bathroom with steam. After stepping inside, I tilt my head back, letting the spray splash my face as the water trickles down my body. My muscles are tense, but that's more from the stress of the campaign than any real hard activity. But tonight, that'll all change.

Having Reagan with me for a few days will be good for our relationship and my enthusiasm on the trail. As the election gets closer, I find myself less in love with the entire process. When I threw my hat into the political ring, I never thought I'd get this far and be vying for the biggest office in the state of Illinois. But I saw all the good I accomplished in the Senate, even though many of the bills I supported were killed by political party bullshit. The governorship would allow me more freedom and possibilities, less encumbered by the bickering from other states, to the detriment of my voters.

I wash up before stepping out, towel-drying quickly, and pull on a pair of loose shorts. I plan to spend the next twelve hours in bed with Reagan, only taking a break to eat. There's nothing I want more than to spend time between my wife's legs, pleasing her and reminding her she's mine.

There's a light knock and a jiggle of the handle before I hear, "Jude."

My heart speeds up as I stalk toward the door and my wife. "Baby," I say as she comes into view, standing in the hallway, looking as beautiful as ever.

I pull her forward, wrapping my arms around her as she drops her bag. She snakes her arms around my neck as she hooks her legs around my back, fastening herself to me. My lips are on hers, hard and quick, needing to feel every inch of her.

"I've missed you," I mutter against her mouth, barely taking a breath before I cover her lips with mine again.

Her fingers tangle in my hair, holding her mouth to mine as her tongue tangles with mine. Our hands move feverishly against each other, needing and wanting the connection. I'm almost breathless when she finally pulls away.

"Hey," she whispers and rests her forehead against mine.

"Hey yourself." I breathe her in, relishing the smell and feel of my wife after so many days.

"I wanna talk before we get lost in bliss for the next however many hours I have you."

My gaze never wavers from her as she speaks. The last thing I want to do is talk, especially when it involves a topic that may lead to another fight. If she didn't think it was going to be an issue, she would've waited to bring it up. That much I know about my wife.

I carry her to the bed, still wrapped around my body, and sit on the edge. She straddles my legs, fidgeting with the ends of my hair near my neck.

"So, talk," I tell her, slipping my fingers under the hem of her dress shirt and stroking the soft skin near her waist.

"Before we go any further, I really want to take this job."

"Okay." I slide my hands up her back, toying with the dip of her spine as she shivers in my arms.

"The good thing is, I don't have to be in Washington as much."

"That's a bonus."

Earlier, when I was only a senator, Reagan being in Washington was great. Now, I'm barely there, but that hasn't cut down on her trips to the city. More than anything, I want more time with my wife. There's a fine line, though. She needs to work, and somehow, I need to learn to accept her absence even if it leaves a bad taste in my mouth.

"So, you'll be home more?" I raise an eyebrow, waiting for her response.

She bites her lip and lowers her gaze. "Well, not exactly."

I take a deep breath, knowing she's about to tell me things I don't want to hear. "Go on."

"Well," she says as her fingernails trace my shoulder blades, sending goose bumps across my skin. "Andrea needs help. She wants someone she trusts and is reliable to help take some of the workload off her shoulders."

I close my eyes and bury my face in the crook of my wife's neck as she continues talking.

"It'll require more short trips, but I'll be able to be home more than before."

"How many trips?" I ask, pressing my lips to her neck near her collarbone.

"One a week at least."

I pull my lips away from her skin and lean back, staring into the eyes of my wife. "You're going to be gone every week?"

The realization of what that means hits me as I repeat the words back to her. As it is, Reagan travels once or twice a month to DC, but she's gone for a week at a time.

"Well, yeah, but they'll be short."

That's always the promise at first. *I'll only be gone a*

*few days.* But days turn into weeks, and time slips away as the hours and workload become more demanding.

"I don't think it's a good idea."

She pushes against my chest, sliding backward off my lap as I try to hold on to her. "Excuse me?" she asks, folding her arms in front of her chest as she stands in front of me, looking down with narrowed eyes. "I didn't say that to you when you said you wanted to be the governor."

"Baby," I say, reaching out and trying to wrap my arms around her again, but she steps backward. My muscles tighten and my agitation swells. "I didn't make the decision to run for governor by myself. We made it together."

"But I didn't stop you."

"I know, but if you had any objections, I wouldn't have entered the race."

"Bullshit." She pulls at her hair and starts to pace. "You were going to do whatever you wanted, even if I didn't like it."

"That's not true." I believe the words as I speak them, but if she had said no, I'm not sure exactly what I would've done. I'd like to think I would've done whatever necessary to keep my wife happy and maintain my career. But would I have gone against her wishes if it was my biggest dream? "This next year is supposed to be about us, Reagan. About starting a family."

"You want me barefoot and pregnant, don't you?

Forget about my job and dreams as long as I'm popping out babies for you?"

My body jerks back as she grows angrier. There's a fire in her I haven't seen in a while.

"Don't make me sound like a macho pig. I just want my wife back."

"Why don't you give up the race and join me on the road? We could see the world together."

"Don't be ridiculous. My work is important."

She points her finger at me with her lips set in a straight line. "That right there is the problem."

Fuck, I wish I could take every word back and stop the shitstorm that has already started to brew in this room like an out-of-control hurricane barreling right for us.

I fucked up. I said the wrong thing, and I now I have to do everything in my power to make that shit right.

"Reagan," I say as she turns her back to me. "Baby, come on." I walk up behind her, wrapping my arms around her waist and pressing my lips to her neck. "I don't want to fight."

She turns her face, looking at me over her shoulder. "I'm taking the fucking job, Jude, and there's nothing you can do to stop me."

11

# REAGAN

THE AIR IN THE ROOM GOES STILL FOR A FEW SECONDS. I can feel Jude's chest moving in and out against my back as he breathes.

I'm surprised he hasn't fired off a comeback yet—he's usually quick on the draw when we're fighting.

He sighs deeply, his hot breath against the skin of my neck sending a tingle down my spine.

"This doesn't need to be decided this instant," he finally says, tightening his hold on me. "We talked about me running for governor for *months* before deciding."

He takes me by the shoulders and turns me to face him, cupping my cheek in one of his massive hands.

"Tonight, let's celebrate the offer and not get out in front of the headlights. Let's just be a husband and wife savoring our time together, okay?"

He knows how to defuse tension when he wants to. It's not just his carefully chosen words that soothe me, but his deep, sexy tone and the way his other hand is cupping my ass.

Without using words, Jude's telling me we've got better things to do tonight than argue. Half of me wants to give in, and half of me wants to tell him he can't distract me with his sex appeal.

"If I want to take this job, I will," I say firmly. "You're not going to fuck me into compliance."

His eyes darken, and the corners of his lips twitch. "Says who?"

"I'm *not* your little woman," I remind him.

Jude's expression turns serious again. "I never said you were, love. You're so much more than that. You're my sun, moon, and stars. My whole world. You know that."

"Then show me. Support me."

He traces his index finger across my jawline. "I do support you, Ray. But I also need you. I can't hire anyone to take your place in my life. If I make it to the governor's mansion, it won't mean shit if you're not there with me. We're a team."

I sigh softly. "I know. I haven't gotten the details on this job yet, though, so I'm not ready to say no."

"I understand. As long as you aren't ready to say yes, either."

"Not right now," I concede. "But I'm very interested, and if it's what I'm hoping, I will want to say yes."

He looks up at the ceiling for an instant, seeming to summon divine intervention.

"Let's talk about it in the morning," he says.

"Uh-huh. After you've gotten off a few times and you're feeling less tense?"

He arches a brow. "I was thinking the same for you, babe."

"A few times, though?" I give him a mock skeptical look. "You think you can make that happen?"

"Oh, little girl." His laugh is low and sexy. "I'm gonna make you so sorry you said that."

He rests his hand on my throat, his thumb stroking my jaw as he kisses me. He's soft and gentle at first, but when I moan into his mouth, he slides his hand down to my breast and squeezes it as his other arm wraps around my waist, pulling me against him.

His mouth is hot and hungry against mine, like he's trying to make up for all the kisses we've missed giving each other in our time apart.

I force myself to pull away from him, licking my lips as I step back and say, "Too bad we don't have the ropes."

"That is a shame, isn't it?" He steps forward and puts his hands around my hips, his eyes swimming with desire as he looks down at me. "You could use a night tied to the bed with your ass in the air."

"Maybe next time." I put my hands on his hard, broad shoulders, squeezing the muscles there.

"Maybe this time." He nods over at the king-size bed where the red nylon ropes stand out against the white bedspread.

A thousand butterflies flap their wings wildly in my stomach. Just the sight of those ropes makes my body respond. I'm warm all over, and I get even warmer when Jude walks over to the bed and picks up the ropes.

Seeing his big, powerful hands holding the restraints reminds me why I'm so turned on by this game we play. I have to trust him completely to let myself be tied up and left helpless. Before Jude, I never trusted any man that way.

But Jude never disappoints me. He pushes our game to the edge of my comfort zone, but never steps past it.

"I could take a nice, long shower first." I glance at the bathroom. "Or soak in the tub for an hour or so."

He shakes his head. "Come here."

I swallow hard, every nerve in my body dancing with awareness as I slip out of my heels and walk over to him.

When I'm right next to him, he turns me around gently, laying my long, dark hair over one of my shoulders to expose the zipper on the simple black dress I'm wearing.

I don't just hear the sliding down of the zipper, I *feel* it. Cool air hits my bare skin, dancing down my back as Jude unzips the dress almost to my waist.

Then his warm hand slides over my shoulder as he slips the dress off of me. It pools at my feet, leaving me in nothing but my lacy red bra and panties.

"One of my favorites," he murmurs, dipping his face to my neck.

His lips are tender as they caress the skin of my neck, his tongue barely grazing my collarbone. My breath comes out in a shaky exhale, all the stress and excitement of the past few days of work melting away.

I can't think about anything but Jude right now. It's nights like this, where he owns me, that I'm free to just *feel*. No thinking. No power plays. No worries about the future. I just give in to the sensations of now, which always threaten to overwhelm me.

"On your back." He speaks into my ear, his tone deep and insistent.

I oblige, feeling powerful as his gaze sweeps over me. Jude would fall to his knees for me if he needed to. He'd walk through fire, slay any dragon, for the sake of our marriage. I know this without a doubt, and that's why I regularly fall to my knees for him.

"I need this so fucking bad," he says as he winds the thin nylon rope around my wrists, binding them together. "You've made me horny as hell with those late-night phone calls."

He ties my wrists to the bed's headboard, and then slides out of the bed, giving me a wolfish smile.

"Spread your legs wide for me, baby."

I do, and he carefully wraps a rope around each of my legs above the ankle, then ties those ropes to the metal bed frame beneath the bed.

I'm breathing hard as he stands up and looks at me.

"You drive me to the edge of sanity, Reagan Titan. I didn't think there was any person I couldn't live without until I met you."

"I could say the same for you."

"You probably shouldn't, though, since you're the one tied up."

He slips his T-shirt off over his head and tosses it to the floor, climbing back onto the bed. Then he leans down to my stomach, his lips grazing over my skin so feather-soft I moan and hold in my breath.

Jude is a patient man, and he takes his time covering every inch of my skin with his mouth. He kisses and caresses with his lips and his breath.

I'm so turned on I'm panting and writhing, twisting against the ropes binding me. It's bliss and agony at the same time.

When he gets out of the bed and stands next to it, his hands slowly pulling his short down, I bite my lip and force myself to stay silent. His lips quirk with a smile.

"It's hard for you, isn't it love?" he says in a teasing tone. "You want to tell me to hurry the fuck up and give you my cock, don't you?"

"Yes," I admit, staring as his shorts fall to the floor, followed by his boxer briefs.

My husband is nothing short of glorious naked. He's hard in every possible way. When he wraps his hand around his shaft and strokes it, I groan in frustration.

"Feels so fucking good." He returns to the bed, on his knees beside me.

All I can do is look up helplessly, my body screaming with arousal, as he strokes himself all the way up and down right next to me.

"I should come on your tits and leave you like this all night," he says in a low growl. "Just to remind you who's boss."

"Jude…no."

He shakes his head and strokes himself faster, groaning with pleasure. "Wrong answer, sweetheart. When we're in bed, there's only one word you need. What is it?"

"Yes." I spit the word out quickly, desperate for him to stop touching himself. "Yes, yes, yes."

He smiles and slows his pace. "That's right."

When his free hand slides between my legs, stroking me through the lace of my panties, I moan loudly and arch my back.

"You want me right here, don't you?" he says in a low tone. "Buried in your pussy."

"Yes. God, yes."

"Can't get your panties off, though, with the ropes." He

shrugs and returns to stroking himself. "And I need to come now."

"Jude!" I pull against the ropes, my arms and legs rising a couple inches off the bed.

"All right, baby." He climbs between my legs. "I'll give your cock-starved pussy what it needs."

He reaches both hands toward my panties, and I feel the lace ripping as he shreds it. Two seconds later, he's inside me, groaning as he sinks every inch in.

His mouth covers mine as he fucks me, kissing me with both reverence and lust. One of his hands wraps around the headboard, and the other cups my cheek as he pounds into me.

Nothing turns me on like being completely at his mercy this way. He's relentless, never slowing down or asking if it's too hard.

Because he knows. After five years of marriage, he knows I love being fucked with everything he's got. And he gives it to me, his expression strained as he holds back when I start to come.

He always makes sure I don't just come, but come long and hard, before he lets himself. Only when I'm giving him a blow job does he let himself come when he wants to.

I yell his name several times and tell him not to stop, though I know he won't. His teeth sink into my shoulder, making me come even harder.

And finally, when he feels me coming down, he slams

into me with all his strength and holds himself there, groaning against my ear as he comes.

He takes a couple seconds just to breathe before kissing me softly. We're both panting and sweaty.

"That was intense," I say softly.

"Yeah." He kisses my brow. My cheeks. My nose. "And much better than fighting, don't you think?"

I laugh as he reaches up to untie my hands.

"Yes. But it's your fault we were fighting, so you should have this conversation with yourself."

He looks down at me. "In the morning, Ray. Tonight, I just want to fall asleep with my wife in my arms. For once."

"Oh, poor Jude Titan." When he frees my first wrist, I reach up and touch his scruffy cheek. "With a wife who doesn't give him his way every time."

He shakes his head as he frees my other wrist. "Don't be surprised if you get woken up by my hand smacking your ass."

I lean up and kiss him. "Don't be surprised if I enjoy it."

He finishes untying me, and I slip into his T-shirt and crawl into bed, snuggling against him.

"Tyson better not come into this room in the morning," I say. "I'll lose my shit if he does."

Jude kisses my forehead. "He's not coming in here, love. He knows better than that."

"I hope so."

"I told my staff that any man who sees you without clothes on, inadvertently or not, will be dick-punched and fired."

"Are you serious?"

"Completely serious. They can come in and out of my room when I'm alone, but not when you're here."

I close my eyes and settle against his warm, solid chest. "I love you, Jude."

"I love you too."

After a few seconds of silence, I say, "I think I should take the job."

"Go to sleep, Reagan," he growls.

I try to, but it takes me a while, because I've got a bad feeling about the conversation we're going to have in the morning.

# 12

# JUDE

I sip my coffee at the small table near the window as Reagan sleeps. She looks so peaceful stretched out across the bed, the sheets tangled around her body as she snores softly. A few times I reached out, ready to wake her, but I let her be. We seem to fight more than anything else anymore, and I'm not ready for a battle at seven in the morning.

I've gone over her job offer a million times in my head. I'm not happy about the entire thing, but she's my wife, and if she's excited, I should be too. I'm greedy, though. I want Reagan at my side and in my bed every night. I don't want her traveling around the world, gone for weeks at a time because Andrea wants time off.

I want my wife, but I know I also want Reagan happy. She gave up her Senate run years ago, and I don't want her to give up on any more dreams. I don't want to be the asshole. Her father did enough to kill her excitement of politics; I don't want to take her zest for life and charity.

I push myself up from the chair, knowing exactly what I need to say as I make my way toward the bed. She stirs with her eyes closed as I climb under the covers and press my front against her bare flesh.

"Hey," she whispers and blinks slowly as she peers over her shoulder at me.

"Hey, baby." I smile, trying to put on my best game face, even though every word of what's about to come out of my mouth is almost a complete lie. "It's so nice waking up with you next to me." Those words are true. What I wouldn't give to do this every day like normal married people.

She rolls over, pressing her breasts against my chest and gives me a lazy little smile. "It is nice, isn't it?"

I rub my nose against her, wishing I could bottle this moment to remember her soft breasts, the heat coming off her silky skin in waves, and the feel of her body in my arms. In a few months, it'll all be just a memory. "I was thinking…" I let my voice drift, not finishing the statement yet.

Her eyebrows rise as she slides her hands up my chest, pulling her face away just enough to see me better. "Yeah?"

"Yeah."

"Good or bad?"

I slowly drag my fingers up her spine, tracing the outline of each bone. "Depends." I'm totally stalling. I don't really want to say the words. They're stuck in my throat, not wanting to come out.

"Jude," Reagan says with the same tone she uses when she's run out of patience.

"I think you should take the job," I blurt, throwing the statement out there much the same way one tears off a Band-Aid from their hairy limb.

She's silent for a moment. Her eyes widen as the realization hits her. The surprise on her face matches how I feel inside, but I don't let the emotion show on my face. There's no taking them back now. No trying to change her mind. Reagan is someone I can't control even if I want to, which I don't.

Her face scrunches, and her fingernails dig into my skin just enough to make me wince. "So help me God, Jude. If you're bullshitting, I will—"

"Baby, I'm not," I interrupt her before she can tell me all the ways she'd make me suffer. "I want you to take the job if it'll make you happy."

She bites her bottom lip and smiles, retracting her claws from my chest. "You just made me the happiest woman in the world."

Her words bring a smile to my face for a second because who doesn't want to see their wife happy. I tell myself to stop being a selfish asshole, something I struggle with sometimes, but only when it comes to her. "That's all I want," I tell her and pull her closer.

She stares up at me like I've just given her the best gift in the world. The happiness radiates from her as she curls into me, giving her lips to me without hesitation. It's like I delivered her the moon and the stars and not a simple nod of approval for her career aspirations. One thing I already knew, Reagan was going to take the position whether or not I wanted her to, so why fight it?

She kisses me slowly as she snakes her arms around my shoulders and starts to toy with the hair at the back of my neck. Goose bumps break out across my skin as I breathe her in.

"Jude." Tyson's voice is like nails on a chalkboard as he repeats my name and knocks on the door.

We break our kiss, staring at each other but not speaking. I gave Tyson explicit instructions not to interrupt Reagan and me. I don't care if the world is coming to an end, I'd rather die in my wife's arms without ever knowing the information in advance.

"Jude. For God's sake, open the door. It's an emergency."

"Ignore him," I say to Reagan, pressing my lips back on hers as she tries to wiggle free from my hold.

"You have to answer him," she tells me as she slides out from under my arms even though I try to stop her.

She slips off the bed and grabs her robe from the back of the chair near the window.

I slam my fist into the mattress before I launch myself upward. "This better be good," I growl as I head toward the door, adjusting my sweats. Every muscle in my body is tense, and my cock isn't too happy about the entire situation either.

"Jude!" Tyson's louder this time, and there's more panic in his voice.

I open the door and lean against it. There's no hint of amusement or happiness on my face either. "What, Tyson?"

He's fully dressed in his business suit, hair perfectly combed like we had a meeting I hadn't remembered. It is way too early to be this pulled together. "Have you seen the news?"

I glance over my shoulder as Reagan walks toward us, tying her robe closed. "Been kind of busy."

Tyson gives Reagan a small smile, but his eyes are quickly back on me. "We need to talk in private."

"She's my wife, Tyson. Not the enemy."

Reagan slides her arm around my side and flattens her palm against my stomach just above the waistband of my shorts. "I promise not to leak a word of whatever you're about to say," she tells him, but she doesn't have to because we don't keep secrets from each other.

Tyson shifts between his feet and blows out a shaky

breath. "We have a major problem." He glances around the hallway and jerks his chin toward the room. "Let me inside."

Reluctantly, I move backward, keeping Reagan behind me, and let Tyson into the one place I thought was going to be a work-free zone for the next so many hours. But as usual, he has a way of spoiling everything.

"What's wrong?" I ask as soon as the door clicks shut.

Tyson paces in front of the window, rubbing his hands together. I haven't seen him this worked up over something in a long time, so whatever it is, it isn't good. "Someone went to the media stating they'll be filing sexual harassment charges against you later today."

His words are like a punch to the gut as I rock backward and wonder if I heard him wrong. "Say that again."

Reagan's clutching my side so tightly, her fingernails are going to leave a mark. "No one will believe her."

"The media's already all over it, Jude. *The Golden Boy Is Going Down* was the last headline I saw come across my phone. There was also *Titan's Tryst*."

"For fuck's sake." I glance toward the ceiling and try to calm myself down before I let my anger get the better of me.

"What do we know? Who is it?" Reagan asks, finally stepping out from behind me.

"I have people trying to find out. Right now, I only know what the media has reported, and it isn't much."

"Maybe she'll just go away."

"I didn't do anything," I say, knowing what a shitstorm this is going to cause in today's political climate. "I've never been inappropriate with anyone on my staff or off."

"I'll get out in front of this," Tyson says.

"You're already behind it if you don't even know who it is," Reagan says sharply. "Get the rest of the team in here *now*."

# 13

# REAGAN

Jude's communications manager has to go. The first moment I get alone with my husband, I'm breaking the news.

Monica is in her late twenties, and she's a social media whiz. She can pump positive stories out there like no one I've ever seen. But right now, we're in crisis mode for the first time, and I can't believe the way she's responding.

"Don't worry about this," she says to Jude for at least the tenth time. "We'll smother it with coverage of what you're doing for veterans."

"This isn't just about *our* feeds," I say from the edge of the couch I'm sitting on. "The media isn't going to run with any of our stuff about veterans' issues right now. It's going to be this story and nothing else."

"But aren't sex scandals a dime a dozen these days?" I

look over to see who said it, and it's an intern casually leaning against a wall. "I say you apologize deeply and don't discuss it again after that."

There's a moment of stunned silence before Jude roars, "I didn't fucking do anything!"

"Babe." I lay a hand on his inked forearm. "Keep it down. We don't want anyone overhearing any of this."

He sighs and leans forward, elbows on his knees and hands in his hair.

"Fuck," he mutters.

I move my hand to his shoulder, which is rock hard with tension.

"You—" Tyson points to the intern "—are here to fetch coffee and learn. No one gives a shit what you think. Don't offer any more opinions unless you're asked to."

The intern nods, his face darkening with embarrassment.

"What the hell is an intern even doing in this room right now?" I ask Tyson.

He puts his hands up in an *I have no idea* gesture.

"I'm loyal," the intern mumbles.

I take a deep breath to steady myself.

"I'm not questioning your loyalty," I say.

I look around at the eight people other than Jude and me who are in the room. Everyone has a somber expression.

"Okay, look. Jude and I need to talk to Tyson alone.

The rest of you set up a base camp in someone's room and start combing through all the news and social media feeds you can find. And get checking with any news sources we have. We need to know who this is and exactly what the allegations are."

Jude nods slightly, still staring at the ground, his shoulders hunched.

Tyson glares at me, his lips pursed. Everyone else quickly files out of the room, and as soon as they're gone, Tyson moves to stand next to the couch Jude and I are sitting on.

"*I'm* in charge of this campaign," he says to me. "You don't order the staff around."

Jude looks up at him, his brow furrowed. "Are you fucking kidding me? Can you save the pissing match for later?"

Tyson focuses on him. "Honestly? No. Our responses to this need to be airtight. We can't be running in different directions. So who's running this show?"

"Me." Jude's tone sends a shiver down my spine. I've rarely heard it, but I know not to push him when he's like this. I hope Tyson does too. "And my wife is my number two, Tyson, not you, so let's just get that straight right now."

Tyson's shoulders drop and he says nothing, but I can see he's still pissed.

"Tyson," I say, running my palm up and down Jude's

back as I speak. "I don't mean any disrespect, truly. I'm just in crisis-response mode, and every minute matters."

"Reagan's thinking straighter than me right now, and she's right," Jude says. "The first thing we have to do is have the conversation, and we don't want anyone in here who doesn't have to be."

Tyson nods, his expression softening. "Okay. I didn't mean any disrespect either, Reagan."

"It's all good. We're all pretty tense right now."

Tyson sits down in the chair across from the couch. "Monica should be in here for this."

Jude shakes his head. "No. She has to go."

I interject. "I completely agree."

"As soon as we're done here, call the RNC and get us a line on some coms crisis people," Jude said. "Veteran people who have weathered this shit before."

Tyson nods silently. "You want me to fire Monica, then?"

Jude considers. "Just demote her. She does great work, but this is way over her head."

"Okay."

Jude turns to face me then, his rumpled dark hair not matching his serious expression. He pulled on a pair of dark gray sweats and a T-shirt when Tyson called this meeting, and he still looks fresh out of bed. We both do. I'm wearing yoga pants and a "Titan for Tomorrow" campaign T-shirt I grabbed.

"I know we have to have this conversation, but—"

"Wait."

My heart hammers with worry over what he's about to say. Did he slip one of those times when I was working and he was lonely? Did he say or do something in a weak moment that he's about to confess to me?

*Not my Jude*, an inner voice says. But there's another inner voice, the one who was devastated by my father's affair, telling me that…maybe. *Maybe.*

I hush both voices, focusing on the business at hand. "Don't you think we need a rec on a strategist from the RNC, too?"

He nods slightly. "I was thinking Janet Fremont."

"She's working for Sheryl Canyon right now."

"Ah, shit." He runs a hand down his scruffy face.

"Jack Carrigan?" Tyson suggests.

"He's good," Jude says with a nod. "See if we can get him. And if not, call the RNC."

"Will do."

Jude turns to me again. "I need you to know I didn't do *anything*, babe."

"I know." The response just comes out automatically, but I can't meet his eyes.

"Guys," Tyson says in a gentle tone. "Let's just get this over with, okay? Let me lead it."

I give him a grateful look and sit back against the

couch, hands in my lap. I really didn't want to interrogate my husband in front of his campaign manager.

"Yeah." Jude takes a sip from his coffee mug and sits back too.

"Have you had any sort of extramarital physical or intimate contact with anyone?" Tyson starts.

"No." Jude's tone is emphatic.

"Ever done anything that could have been construed as nonconsensual? And remember, this doesn't have to be recent. This could be a woman saying you did something inappropriate ten years ago."

Jude shakes his head. "No. Even before I was married, I never forced myself on anyone. That's against everything I am."

"Every done any sort of role-playing with a partner?"

Jude sighs heavily. "No, not really. There was a woman who wanted to call me Daddy back when I was in the Corps, that's about it. It was just a one-night thing."

My stomach twists at the visual his words give me. I hate the idea of my husband screwing *any* other woman, even if it was before we met.

"You good, Reagan?" Tyson asks me.

"I'm fine."

He continues. "Ever had sex with someone video-recorded?"

Jude shakes his head. "Not that I'm aware of."

"Ever gotten a woman pregnant?"

My stomach rolls with nausea at the very thought.

"No." Jude puts a palm on my thigh.

"Not to your knowledge, anyway," Tyson says, looking sheepish.

"I guess. It'd be a complete fucking shock, though."

I swallow hard, my mind racing with possibilities. Just an hour ago, my biggest worry was whether Jude would get on board with my job offer. And now…I'm thinking about the possibility that my husband could have a child out there that he never knew about.

*I* want to have his babies. Our babies. The thought of another woman having his baby makes me…

Tearful. I have to fight back the tears. I almost can't breathe for a second.

"Babe." Jude looks into my eyes. "I swear to you, there's nothing…*nothing*."

"I…I know." My voice shakes.

"Any woman you've ever rejected who may feel scorned?" Tyson presses.

Jude sighs deeply. "I mean…ever? Sure, I've rejected women."

Tyson makes a note in the small notebook he always carries.

"Any woman you've ever tried to get with who wasn't interested?"

"Again"—my husband's voice is agitated—"ever? Of course."

"These are the people we have to be considering before we know more," Tyson says. "You know how these things are."

"I know." Jude blows out a breath. "This is nothing, I guarantee it. But that doesn't stop someone from making an accusation that could cost me my career. My honor."

"All we can do for now is hunker down and wait to see what breaks," Tyson says. "You guys can't leave this room for now."

I nod, my head spinning. Tyson stands up and looks down at us.

"Think about it and talk about it with Reagan," he says. "You know the drill—anything you think of, let me know so we can try to get out in front of it. I'll come update you guys when we get any details."

"Thanks," Jude says solemnly.

We both stand as Tyson leaves the room, and then Jude turns to me, his dark eyes swimming with emotion.

"I can't believe this is happening," he says softly.

"It'll be okay."

"You believe me, right? I can't do any of this without you beside me. I need to know you believe me."

"I do, but—"

"But?" His eyes bulge with disbelief.

"But like Tyson said, this could be something from your past. Someone you turned down who wants revenge. We just don't know what we're dealing with yet."

He nods and closes his eyes for a second, then walks toward me and puts his hands on my hips. "You can't leave me, Ray. I've never been through anything like this, and I have to have you with me."

"Well, Tyson quarantined us to this room, so…" My small attempt at humor falls flat.

"I mean after we get news, too. This changes everything. I need you by my side."

To show the world he has a devoted wife. Memories of my father's sex scandal hit me so hard, I feel like the wind has been knocked out of me.

"I'm here," I say softly.

He takes me into his arms then, and I rest my cheek against his chest. His solid warmth envelops me for a few sweet moments, but then the nightmare comes blaring back into my consciousness.

I know Jude has been faithful to me. But this whole thing still sickens me in a way no one else would understand.

I have to live the nightmare again. The questions. The judgment. The condemnation.

True or false, this accusation against my husband is going to change everything.

# 14

# JUDE

"WE SHOULD CANCEL TONIGHT," TYSON SAYS AFTER HE comes back into our room.

"Any leads?" I ask, ignoring his statement.

There's no way I'm canceling any events or campaign stops. I refuse to let the liars win. They can try to bring down my campaign—it won't be the first time—but I know I am in the right. I will not be making a statement of apology in order to sweep the accusation under the rug either. I did nothing wrong and refuse to give them any more power than they already seem to hold.

Tyson rubs his face with his palms and groans. "Nothing," he replies, moving his hands away and dropping his arms as if he's been defeated. "I don't get it. Everyone is being so tight-lipped."

"Then right now, I call bullshit on the entire thing. If someone had truly made the allegation, they would've come forward by now," I tell him as I move across the room to help Reagan with her coat.

"Don't be so quick to dismiss it, Jude," Reagan says as she shrugs on the coat and turns to face me. "The fact that every media outlet is talking about it is all the credibility needed to bring down the campaign."

"She's right," Tyson adds and winces like the words are bitter on his tongue.

There's still no love lost between Reagan and Tyson. I don't think there ever will be. They'll forever be at odds, both politically and personally, and the two will never find middle ground for very long.

Tyson takes a step toward us as I grab my suit jacket from the closet. "Jude, I beg you to change your mind about going to this event."

I hold up my hand, stopping him before he can say another word. "We're going, Tyson. Either earn your pay and manage this shit, or I'll find someone who will."

"Hey." Reagan touches my chin and turns my face toward her. "There's no one better than Tyson. You need to calm down. He's doing his job by giving you his opinion. Everyone here knows you're going to do what you want, but he has every right to say what he did."

I blow out a breath and close my eyes for a moment.

I'm on edge and ready to pounce, but I'm taking it out on the wrong people. Reagan stares at me, waiting for me to respond or probably apologize to Tyson for overreacting.

"I'm sorry, Tyson," I say, and even though the words are coming out of my mouth, the tone doesn't convey an ounce of apology. "I know you're only giving me advice, but I'm going tonight. I will not cave."

Tyson throws up his hands and grunts, "Fine." He grumbles under his breath about me never listening as he follows us out the hotel room.

The ride down in the elevator is tense. Tyson's standing in front of us, staring at the lights above the door as we descend. He's unusually quiet but probably so aggravated with me

Reagan's at my side, stroking my back underneath my jacket. I lean over, bringing my mouth right next to her ear, and whisper, "You look beautiful tonight."

She smiles up at me and winks, just as beautiful as the first time I laid eyes on her. It seems like more than five years ago since our paths first crossed, but not because of our relationship. That's been the best part of the last five years.

When the elevator stops, Tyson steps out and turns toward us. "At least go out the back entrance of the hotel. The media is camped out in the front."

"Come on, Tyson." I place my hand on the small of

Reagan's back, ushering her away from the hotel's front lobby. "We'll listen to you for once. We have a party to get to, and we're already late."

The annual gala and charity silent auction for the American Ammunitions Association is one of the biggest conservative events of the year. It's always heavily attended by the biggest names in the Republican party and some of the wealthiest people in the state. It's the event to be seen at if you're anyone of importance, and with this being so close to election day, I have to be in attendance.

The car's already waiting for us in the rear, and I give Tyson a smirk before climbing in the back. "You have me all figured out, don't you?"

"I've known you a lot of years, Jude." He places his elbow on the armrest and stares out the window for a moment as the car starts to pull away from the curb. "Let's talk about how we're going to handle any questions."

Reagan curls into my side as I rest my hand on her knee. "Do you think people are going to say anything to me?" My thumb slides across her velvety skin, and it pebbles underneath my touch.

"Some asshole will say something," Reagan says. "You know how these rich pricks are, Jude."

"I'll handle them, but I'm not giving an official statement."

"Try to keep the conversation moving. Any moment of

silence and it'll be their chance to slip it in." Tyson pulls out his phone, typing feverishly with his tongue peeking out from between his lips.

"What's wrong?" I ask, knowing Tyson better than almost everyone else in my life. The man has so many tells, and I've made sure to study them all.

"We may have a lead," he tells me but doesn't look up. "But nothing solid."

"Who?" Reagan asks, shifting in her seat.

Tucking his phone into his jacket pocket, Tyson finally makes eye contact. "Wasn't given a name yet. Just told to stand by for more information soon."

"I want to know as soon as you do," I say, trying to remove all anger from my voice. My pulse is jumping, my temper flaring, and somehow, I have to walk into the hotel event room with a smile on my face.

Reagan places her hand over mine, stroking my skin softly. "I won't leave your side tonight," she reassures me.

I've always felt like anything was possible as long as Reagan was by my side. I've never fought a campaign without her. "Tyson," I say to get his attention as the car pulls up along the sidewalk in front of the hotel. "Why don't you get out and give us a few minutes alone?" My hand tightens on Reagan's leg as she opens her mouth and starts to speak. "We'll be quick, but I need some time with my wife."

Tyson nods before he opens the door. He has one foot out when he turns and says, "Don't be too long. People will be asking about you."

I nod, but I don't bother to speak to him. "Sir," I call out, and the driver looks at me in the rearview mirror, "drive around until I tell you to stop."

"Anything you'd like, Mr. Titan. Would you like some privacy, sir?"

"Yes, please."

"Jude," Reagan whispers as the black glass slides up, giving us complete privacy. "I don't know…"

I place my finger against her lips. "I need some time with you and only you, Reagan. Don't deny me this."

She nods slowly and doesn't put up much of a fight as I grab her around the waist and lift her into my lap. "I want to touch you," I say, staring into my wife's eyes. "I need to touch you."

She squirms as I slide my hand up her leg, moving past her knee and inner thigh before finding the edge of her panties. "Jude," she whispers again, but it's not for me to stop.

I know that burning in her eyes and the longing in her voice. She wants my touch as much as I need to give it to her. I lean in, sealing my lips over hers and soak in her moans as my fingertips slip underneath the lace.

She turns her upper body toward me, giving me more

of her mouth and slides her legs apart as I push her panties to the side. My cock hardens underneath her ass, and I'd love more than anything to bury myself inside of her, but there's not time for that with the crowd waiting for us at the hotel. I just needed her mouth, her pleasure, to get me through the next couple hours of political games.

Her tongue swirls around mine, greedy and sure, as she melts into me. My touch is light, sweeping over her soft skin, making her groan because Reagan has never been one to take anything slow. But I won't let her control my speed. No amount of complaining is going to make me move faster.

Her kiss grows more demanding as my fingers circle around her clit. She shivers in my arms with every passing sweep over her sensitive skin. She's already wet, wanting every bit of this as much as I do.

I slide my fingers down, pushing two slowly inside her, and stroke her clit. She moans into my mouth, feeding me air, and I take it. Her pussy contracts around my fingers, begging for more each time I pull them out before thrusting them in a little deeper.

She breaks the kiss and stares at me with her lips parted. "Jude," she says softly as her eyes roll back. "I need your cock."

"There's no time," I tell her, keeping my rhythm steady, finger-fucking her just how she likes it.

"We can be quick. I'll get on top." She smirks. "Undo your pants," she says as she slides off me and pulls her panties off from underneath her dress.

I'm not going to argue with that. I lift my ass, unzipping my pants before pulling them down to my ankles. Before I've even eased back into the seat, Reagan's already straddling me with my hard cock in her hands.

"Just relax," she says, rubbing the tip of my dick through her wetness. "Let me make you feel good."

I grab her hips, holding her dress around her waist as she eases herself down my shaft. I groan, blowing out a breath as her warmth envelops me and sends a shiver down my spine. The jostling of the car adds to the sensations as she rises up and lowers herself again.

Over and over, she fucks me, bucking in my lap before crashing her lips down on mine. My fingertips dig into her hips as I try to control her speed, but Reagan's too amped up to control. In this position, riding my cock, she's dominating me, and I'm strangely okay with it. More than okay. I'm loving it.

She grinds her cunt against me as she impales herself, moving faster until the orgasm crashes over us both. Her kiss softens, the strokes of her tongue growing gentler as the aftershocks rake over us.

"Thanks," she says, leaning her forehead against mine.

I smile at my wife and kiss her lips one more time. "I love you," I say and leave it at that.

There's nothing more that needs to be said. There's no one who completes me the way Reagan does. There's no more calming force in my life than having my wife at my side. Sex or no sex, she's it for me.

# 15

# REAGAN

Two hours later, I'm really glad Jude initiated that hot sex on the way here. The only things keeping me relaxed right now are the orgasm I had in the car and the glass of Merlot in my hand.

"You are every bit as lovely as I've heard," an older man says as his eyes rake over my body. "You're a lucky man, Jude."

"Yes, I am." My husband's tone is clipped. "And a protective one as well."

The warning in his tone goes unnoticed by the half-drunk guy in an expensive suit. He laughs and keeps ogling me as he says, "If that was mine, I'd be protective too."

I press a palm to Jude's back, trying to calm him. This

comes with the territory, and we both know it. But Jude's temper is shorter than usual right now.

Tyson finally got the details of the allegations against Jude confirmed about an hour ago, and we all huddled in a conference room for five minutes so he could tell us.

The woman's name is Jessica Culbertson, and she's a twenty-five-year-old aspiring model. She alleges that she was getting a photo taken with Jude at an event two months ago and he grabbed her ass and invited her back to his room, then got hostile and threatened her when she refused.

Even though I felt shattered that someone would make an accusation like that against Jude, I held it together. I don't want anyone, even Tyson, to know how much I'm struggling with all of this.

Most of all, I don't want Jude to know. He'll think I doubt him, and it's not that. Even as Tyson spelled out the allegations Jessica is lodging against Jude, I knew he hadn't done any of it.

Jude's not the sort to touch any woman who doesn't want him to. He's never had to, because women take one look at him and line up in hopes he'll notice them.

When we're apart, my husband lets me know in no uncertain terms how sexually frustrated he is. He gets pretty moody about it.

It's the humiliation factor that has me feeling this way. Everything my family went through when my father's affair came out has come rushing back. Even tonight, I'm getting looks of pity and disdain, and these are Jude's supporters.

For once, I'm glad to see Tyson. He excuses Jude and me from the drunken asshole we're standing with and leads us back to the conference room we met in before.

"Statement's ready," he says, passing Jude a piece of paper.

Jude scans it, then passes it to me. I read each word carefully as Jude asks Tyson, "Who wrote it?"

"I did. Since we don't have a coms leader right now, I figured—"

"It's good," Jude cuts in.

I finish reading and nod in agreement. "You said what needed to be said and nothing more. It's a clear, concise denial."

Tyson nods, then levels his gaze at Jude.

"I have a photo of the accuser." He passes Jude his phone, and Jude looks down at the screen. "Any memory of meeting her at any point?"

Jude shakes his head. "She doesn't look familiar, but you know how campaigning goes. I see so many people every day. She could have been at an event, and I don't remember it. But if she was, I definitely didn't touch her or proposition her."

Tyson nods and tucks the written statement back inside

a folder. "We'll get this released. How long do you want to hang here?"

"Another hour should be good," Jude says, putting an arm around my waist.

Jude turns for the door then, and I put a hand on his arm to stop him.

"Hey, Tyson, can you give us a minute alone?" I ask.

"Sure." He steps out of the room and closes the door behind him.

Jude put his hands on my waist and pulls me close, looking down into my eyes. "What's up?"

"My bosses have been blowing up my phone with texts about this. I'm not sure what to tell them."

Jude furrows his brow in confusion. "What do you mean? Tell them it's bullshit."

I sigh softly. "That's not the issue. They're concerned with perception. It's hard for me to work on bipartisan issues when Democrats are flaming pissed at you."

"Democrats are *always* flaming pissed at me, love."

"Not like this. There are even Republican women calling for a full investigation."

Jude's expression darkens. "Bring on an investigation. I have nothing to hide because I didn't do anything."

"I know." I lay a palm on his chest. "But you get where they're coming from, right?"

He shakes his head. "Sounds like they're blaming you

for the shitstorm surrounding me, and that's bullshit. You're your own person."

"I know, but we're married."

He considers for a second before saying, "Aren't you planning on quitting anyway? To take the job with Andrea?"

I nod and look down at the floor. "I was, but…Andrea rescinded her offer. I just saw the text when I checked my phone a few minutes ago."

Jude's eyes widen with disbelief. "What the fuck? Over this?"

"I'm sure it is. Andrea's work is much like the Lancet Foundation's. She can't have the optics of a sex scandal."

"Fuck." Jude rubs his temple and exhales deeply. "There is no sex scandal, Ray."

"I know." I overemphasize the words, frustrated with him telling me what we both already know. "But it's about perception, Jude."

"No, this is total bullshit. You've busted your ass for the Lancet Foundation, and now they want you to resign over a bullshit accusation against *me*? With no proof at all?"

"They want me to take a leave of absence."

"Is that what you want?"

I shrug. "I think it's for the best. I'd end up getting cornered with questions about you in any meetings I have anyway. And I get why the Lancet people need to distance themselves from us."

Jude starts to speak, stops himself, and then starts again. "No, babe. Fuck no. That's not okay. You live in this world where everyone has to look out for number one, because that's what your dad always did."

I recoil. "Excuse me?"

"I don't mean you. I mean the people around you. You don't think you deserve loyalty. But you do, Reagan. You fucking do. You were loyal to that organization, and if any of them were worth a shit, they'd be loyal to you."

"Politics isn't always fair, though. We both know that."

He runs a hand through his dark hair, his jaw set in a tense line. "Yeah, but it's not supposed to affect my wife. Your career that you've worked so hard for… Fuck." He shakes his head and looks away.

"Hey." I use my fingertips to turn his cheek until he's facing me. "This is where I need to be right now anyway. Let's focus on the biggest fire, and we'll worry about the other little ones later."

He nods solemnly. "I do need you here. I don't know why this woman made up that story, but I know her reason can't be good. This could ruin me."

"We're not going there," I say firmly. "We're going to take this campaign one day at a time. We knew going in that it would be a fight."

"Yeah." He wraps his arms around me and pulls me close. "But I should've been the only one at risk, not you."

"This stuff never just touches the candidate—it touches the entire family."

His deep sigh ruffles my hair. "You know that better than anyone. You've been through this once already."

His tone is laced with guilt. And while that's not what I want him to feel, there's a sense of relief that he gets it. I didn't have to tell him how hard this is for me, because he knows me well enough to get it.

"My dad was guilty, though, and you aren't," I remind him.

"Yeah, but in the court of public opinion, I'm guilty until proven innocent."

"One day at a time," I remind him. "There's no evidence that you did what she says, but there may be evidence that you didn't. Let's let it play out."

He tightens his hold on me. "No matter who we bring on for communications and strategy, you and I get the final say on everything. I trust your judgment more than anyone's."

I close my eyes, my lips curving up in a smile. It feels good to hear him say those words, even after all this time together.

"We'll be okay," I say softly. "No matter what happens, we'll be okay."

"I hear you, babe, I really do." His tone is defeated.

"But integrity is everything to me. I don't care if I lose fairly, as long as I worked my hardest. But this… Fuck, I really don't want to go down like this."

I press my cheek to his chest, wishing I had words of reassurance. But I don't. If these charges can't be proven false, Jude won't recover from being accused of sexual harassment. Even if he wins the race and becomes governor, having his honor questioned will last forever for him.

# 16

# JUDE

"In closing, I vehemently deny the allegations against me. I'm a man of my word, and as a Marine, my honor is everything to me. I never touched the woman in question, nor any woman, in a suggestive or inappropriate manner. I may be a senator and running for the governorship, but above all else, I'm a devoted and loyal husband." I step back from the podium as reporters rise to their feet, hurling questions like they hadn't heard a word of my official statement.

This is the dirty side of politics. The reason why so many good people who could really help better our country stay far away. Everyone has a skeleton or two in their closet, but no one wants to risk that indiscretion becoming public knowledge. Then there are the lies that are created to damage a person's creditability. Planting the seed in any voter's mind is dangerous.

The one thing I know is that I never touched that woman or any woman besides my wife in well over five years. I never even thought about having an affair. But that didn't stop the lies from landing on my doorstep.

"You were fabulous," Reagan says as she wraps her arms around my stomach as soon as I make my way backstage, and she hugs me tightly. "I couldn't have done it better myself."

I kiss the top of her head, closing my eyes so I can forget everything around me for just a moment. I try to block out the low murmur of the reporters in the other room as they scramble to get their story submitted for the evening news. Tyson's on the phone, yelling at someone about something I probably don't even want to know about.

"I love you," I whisper into her hair and take a deep breath, losing myself in her familiar scent. "I don't know what I'd do without you."

There's nothing but truth in that statement. She's my other half, the feisty liberal half, but still vital in everything I am and will continue to be.

She tilts her head back and stares up at me. "You'll never get rid of me, Jude."

In the last five years, I've seen marriages end for much less than a simple allegation. Distance spent apart is usually the crushing factor, but I refuse to let any of it do us in. When I said my vows and promised *until death do us part,* I meant every single word.

I take a deep breath and utter the words I never wanted to say, "Should I drop out?"

Her eyes widen as she leans back, staring at me in disbelief. "You will do no such thing. That's admitting defeat, and in a way, proving to the world you're guilty. You will *not* drop out of this race. Do you understand?"

I nod and somehow manage a smile. "I don't want to drop out, but I would for you, Reagan. Only for you."

There's nothing I wouldn't do for my wife, including giving up my career in politics if I knew it would make her happy. If there were any chance my career would destroy our marriage, I'd give my resignation and never look back without a single thought or regret.

She slides her hands to my front, placing her palms against my chest. "I can take the heat, especially when I know they're lies. You fight and don't stop until you're sitting in the governor's office."

"*We're* sitting in the governor's office," I remind her.

This isn't a one-man show. To the public, it may be, but I value Reagan's advice even though I don't always take it. We may be polar opposites on almost every issue, but she helps me understand the other side of the argument. She's the biggest asset to my political career even if the people around me don't see it that way.

"Have faith that it'll all work out."

She's always so upbeat and somehow believes in the good. But I've seen too much of the bad win in this world, including her father, to allow myself to buy into any fairy tales.

Tyson stalks across the backstage area, clutching his phone in his hands. "We may have gotten a break."

"What?" My fingers tighten on Reagan's side as I gaze over her head. "How?"

"There's a lot of video footage from the event in question. My people are scouring every moment, trying to find the few moments you spent with her. If we can show proof, people can no longer take her claim seriously, and we can move forward."

Of course. I hadn't even thought about the dozens of reporters and the hundreds of supporters in attendance, all taking video and photos from every angle possible. There's never a moment of a rally that isn't on tape in some shape or form. There has to be something to prove my innocence, or at least, I hope there is… God, I hope there is.

"Good work, Tyson." Reagan turns in my arms and smiles at him. Their new respect for each other is nice but unsettling at the same time.

"Hopefully, they'll find something on the tapes," I say.

"If you met her, it'll be on them. I had cameras everywhere. Plus, your supporters all had their phones out. If it happened, someone would've taken a photo or video," Tyson tells us.

"It didn't happen," I repeat because, for some reason, I feel like Tyson hasn't believed me.

"I know. I know." He nods slowly before pursing his lips. "We're going to crush that bitch."

"Tyson," I hiss. "Don't ever use that demeaning language with me and especially not in front of my wife."

"No." Reagan turns her face toward me. "She is a bitch."

"Okay. Okay. So now we wait and hope we have something to vindicate me."

"Yeah," Tyson says with a sigh. "This should all be over in forty-eight hours."

*From his mouth to God's ears.*

"Let's get lost for the evening," Reagan says to me, running her palms up my bare forearms. "What do you say?"

I glance over at Tyson, waiting for him to object, but he waves me off. "I thought you'd never ask," I tell her and move toward the doorway, holding her hand, without so much as a backward glance.

***

MY HANDS ARE over her eyes as we enter the hotel room. During dinner, I slipped away and had everything set up in the penthouse I rented for the night. I didn't want Tyson to be able to find us, and I wanted the evening to be more special than it would've been in our normal hotel suite.

"Why won't you let me see?" she asks as the door closes behind us, sealing us away from any prying eyes and the world outside.

"One second," I tell her with my mouth next to her ear. My eyes sweep across the room, making sure everything is perfect. I'm actually surprised the concierge was able to pull everything off so quickly down to the last detail. "Now that we're here, no more talking about anything except us. Are we clear?"

She shivers in my arms as my breath skids across her skin. "Yes, Jude," she replies in a small, soft voice. "I understand."

"This is about us. About pleasure. About nothing more than a husband and wife. There's nothing but this moment. This room. The feeling of your skin against mine. No sounds other than moans of pleasure."

Her lips are parted as she listens to me speak, but she nods, understanding every bit of what I mean. This is how I unwind, how I close myself away and forget that I'm anything more than a hungry man in love with my wife.

I move my hands away from her face, showing her the room with the floor-to-ceiling windows overlooking the town in the swankiest hotel money could buy in this part of Illinois.

She looks around, her eyes moving from the windows to the hundreds of flickering candles around the room. "It's beautiful," she whispers as I stroke the soft skin on her bare shoulders.

"No one can find us. I made sure of it," I tell her, slowly easing down the straps of her dress.

The material falls away, pooling on the carpet around her feet. I run my fingers up her arms, causing goose bumps to break out across her flesh.

"Tonight's mine, Reagan. You're mine. I want to lose myself in you." I press my lips to her neck, placing them over her pulse. "Use you every way I can until my body and yours can't take any more."

# 17

# REAGAN

Tonight, there are no worries about the accusations against my husband. I'm not thinking about the loss of my job or Andrea's offer.

There's nothing on my mind right now but pleasure. Jude's mouth is making its second pass up and down my legs, a nip on my inner thigh causing me to moan in response.

We haven't spoken since falling into this bed together. Unless my fragmented cries of pleasure count, that is. Jude spent at least thirty minutes bringing me to the edge of release with his mouth between my legs, deliberately slowing when I was almost there.

When he finally let me come, tears pricked at the corners of my eyes from the intensity.

He only gave me a minute to recover before he pinned

my hands to the mattress over my head, one of his hands easily trapping both of mine. He cupped my ass and fucked me fast and hard, his groan vibrating against my skin as he came.

We lay with our legs wrapped around each other for a while after that, just tracing invisible lines on each other's sweaty skin, basking in the quiet and calm.

Jude and I get very little peaceful time together. Our schedules are usually frenzied, and lately, we've both been exhausted as soon as it's time to sleep.

Tonight is reminding me what matters most in my life —not politics or parties, not jobs or poll numbers—my husband.

We never got a blissful, storybook beginning to our marriage. With Jude being a senator, we only took enough time to get married and escape for a quick honeymoon.

After that, we both got to work proving to voters and supporters that we weren't crazy for falling in love. We felt an obligation to prove ourselves, and I don't know that we've ever really stopped.

"Mmm, I don't think I can handle any more of that," I murmur as Jude's warm breath brushes across the apex of my thighs.

He lets out a deep note of amusement before running the tip of his tongue between my lips, opening them just enough to elicit a ragged moan from me.

"Sure you can," he says, his dark eyes meeting mine.

The sight of him staring intensely at me from between my thighs sends a tingle of arousal from the top to the base of my spine.

"Um…maybe," I manage.

Jude bites the sensitive skin of my inner thigh gently. "I'll hold you down if I have to, Mrs. Titan."

His tongue delves deeper, and I sigh with pleasure as he explores every spot still sensitive from the last freight train orgasm he gave me.

This night is turning out to be everything I didn't even know I needed. Jude knew, though. It's heaven having a man who sometimes knows me better than I know myself.

---

A COUPLE HOURS LATER, we slip out of bed to order room service. While we're waiting, Jude cracks open the curtains, and we look out over the small city, many of the night lights already dark.

I slip on a white silk robe and wrap my arms around his waist, closing my eyes as I soak in his warm, solid presence.

"I love you," I say, pressing a soft kiss to his chest.

"I love you too." He wraps his arms around me. "Thanks for being my rock through all of this."

"Anytime. For better or worse, right?"

He kisses the top of my head. "You really think it's all

gonna be worth it? All the time apart? Not having a regular life in our home? That's all I ever wanted when I was in the service, you know. A person and a place to be my home."

"Well, you have the person." I kiss his chest again. "And we have the place. We're just away from it right now."

"Yeah, but…" He sighs softly. "If I win, we'll have to move in to the governor's mansion. Chicago's our home, though."

"We'll split our time."

He leans back and looks down into my eyes.

"Tell me you'll be content being a governor's wife. Is that enough for you?"

"Who says that's all I'll be? I've got options."

"I know, babe, but having you gone all the time…" He turns to look out the window. "I just wonder if it's the right thing for us. I don't want to keep moving in to a bigger and better office if it costs us our life together. If our kids will be splitting time between homes and not having the life we want for them. Always under scrutiny like we are."

"You get used to it," I say softly. "I did."

"Do you ever wish we had a…simpler life? Where we could just go have a drink or dinner without photographers chasing us?"

"Sure," I admit. "But with great privilege comes great responsibility."

I follow Jude's gaze out to the few twinkling lights left. We stay like that, lost in our own thoughts, until the room service knock sounds on the door.

And as we eat, sadness about the night ending sets in. After this, we'll go back to bed, and I'll be asleep soon. Then when we wake up, it'll be back to the campaign trail grind.

I needed this night to remind me what matters most. And I wish we could have more nights like this. But for now, it's a luxury.

---

THE NEXT AFTERNOON, I'm finishing up lunch with a member of the *Chicago Tribune's* editorial board when my phone rings.

"Talk soon," Elaine Hammond says, hugging me quickly and excusing herself so I can take the call.

I slide my finger across the screen to answer. "Hey, Mom. How are you?"

"Oh, I'm okay. How's campaign life?"

"Oh, you know. Busy."

There's an awkward pause, because she *does* know. My mom spent more than thirty years as the dutiful, smiling wife of a senator before being crushed by news of my father's affair and secret family.

"You're doing okay with it, though, right?" she asks.

"Oh, yeah." I look from side to side, weighing whether it's safe to speak frankly in a restaurant full of people, and think better of it. "I just finished a lunch, so I'm at a restaurant."

"Ah. I understand."

I get up and sling my bag over my shoulder, heading for the restaurant's entrance. "Mom, are you okay? You sound nasal, like you've been crying."

I furrow my brow with concern. My mom and I are always open with each other, and I can tell she's not okay.

"What's going on? Tell me."

She sighs heavily. "You know, it's probably nothing."

"What's probably nothing?"

"I had my routine mammogram, and I had to go back for a follow-up. They want to do a biopsy of a lump in my breast."

I reach out for something to stabilize myself as light-headedness sets in. My hand lands on the rim of a huge indoor planter inside the restaurant's lobby.

"A lump? There's for sure a lump?"

"Yes. I thought about waiting to tell you until the results are in, but—"

"Mom, no. Why didn't you tell me when you had to go back for a second scan?"

"It may be nothing, Reagan. The doctor will know more after the biopsy."

I can't cry, though it's all I want to do right now. I've

never even considered anything bad happening to my mom. The poor woman's been through so much already thanks to my father.

"I want to be there with you." I sink down onto the wooden bench next to the plant, swallowing against the knot in my throat.

"Honey, I'm okay. You and Jude have your hands full right now."

"Don't be ridiculous." My tone is outraged because I can't give in to what I'm really feeling, or I'll burst into tears. "Who's there with you? Is Abby there?"

"Your sister is still on assignment in Europe. I don't need anyone here with me."

"Well, I'm coming anyway. When is the biopsy?"

After a pause, she says, "Wednesday."

Two days away. I close my eyes and steady myself.

"I'm booking the soonest flight out. I'll text you my landing time. Can you pick me up?"

"Of course."

"I love you, Mom. I'll be there soon."

"I love you too, you headstrong girl."

I end the call and log on to a travel site, finding a flight that leaves in two hours. It's nonstop to Miami, where my mom lives by herself in a modest beach house.

As soon as my travel is booked, I text Jude, telling him I'm going. I don't really even have time to go back to the campaign bus and pack a bag. I can borrow clothes from my mom or pick a few things up when I get there, though.

All I care about right now is getting to my mom as soon as possible. I walk outside and hail a cab, steeling myself.

I can't fall apart. My mom needs me.

Jude texts back.

**Jude: Babe, I'm so sorry. What can I do?**

**Me: I don't think there's anything, but thanks for offering. I don't know when I'll be back. I won't be able to do that luncheon thing Thursday.**

**Jude: Don't worry about anything, I'll have staffers cancel your stuff. Do you need me to come with you? I will.**

**Me: I know. Thanks. I'll be okay.**

**Jude: Let me know when you land, okay?**

**Me: Okay.**

**Jude: Love you more than anything.**

**Me: You too.**

I slide into the waiting cab and ask the driver to take me to O'Hare. On the drive, I open a browser on my phone to check my Google alerts for anything on Jude's campaign.

The headline I see stops me cold: *Secret Titan Tryst?*

Oh, hell no. This is the last thing we need right now. I click on the link, my heart pounding uncontrollably as the page loads.

My gaze goes right to the photo. It's Jude, his face partially covered but recognizable between two long curtains in front of a floor-to-ceiling window. His arms are wrapped around the waist of a woman whose dark hair conceals her face.

I can't help but laugh, because it's *me*. Jude's "tryst" was our night at the hotel the other evening. The photo looks like it was shot from a building across from us as we waited for our room service to arrive.

For fuck's sake. Those reporters need to find some actual stories to work on.

1 8

# JUDE

TYSON'S ABOUT TO FUCKING COMBUST. RIGHT HERE IN front of me, I swear the guy's gonna just burst into flames.

"How can they not do any follow-up whatsoever? This is complete bullshit. They owe us a retraction on the same page they ran that phony story."

I shrug. "I guess, in their minds, they weren't wrong. I was having a tryst. It was just with my wife."

He shakes his head vehemently. "Men don't have *trysts* with their wives. The word implies something illicit and clandestine."

I push a few buttons on my phone screen. "Tryst—a private, romantic rendezvous between lovers. Yeah, that's what it was."

Filthy sex is romantic, right? I smile to myself as I remember the night spent between my wife's thighs.

"Why are you so cool about this?" Tyson demands. "On the heels of the Culbertson accusation, this could be the one-two punch that ends this campaign."

I shrug. "I'll own up to a tryst with my wife any day of the week. There's a right-wing talk show host who called me earlier and asked to interview me about it."

"Don't do it." Tyson's eyes widen. "He'll question you about the Culbertson thing, too."

"I hope he does. I have nothing to hide because I did nothing wrong." I clap him on the shoulder. "Relax, Tyson. This shit's a marathon, not a sprint. The talk show host is a good friend of the Branch brothers. This is gonna be a softball interview."

He exhales deeply. Poor Tyson. His clothes are wrinkled, and his hair is getting grayer by the day.

"You need a day off, man," I tell him.

"A day off? Are you kidding me? In the middle of all this?"

I nod. "It's nothing the rest of us can't handle for a day."

"Glad to know I'm needed," he grumbles.

"You *are* needed. That's why I want you to take a day to recharge. Have some fun. Eat some food you don't have to shovel into your mouth in five minutes or less on the bus. Put on some clean clothes, maybe."

He glances down at his shirt. "My clothes look dirty?"

I shrug a shoulder. "A little wrinkled, maybe."

"I slept in these clothes last night," he admits.

"You slept in those clothes the night before last, too."

"Oh, shit. Did I really?"

"Tyson, if I see your face in the next twenty-four hours, you're fired."

His lips quirk in a smile, followed quickly by a skeptical expression. "Really?"

I nod. "Get your ass out of here, man. I've got this."

He takes out his phone and looks at the screen. "Oh, shit. Maybe another day."

"What is it?"

He turns the screen to face me. There's a posed photo of me smiling with one man and three women. Looks like it was taken at a recent rally. I arch my brows at Tyson in question.

"The woman to your immediate left is Jessica Culbertson," he says. "Looks like a blogger located it before the people I hired could."

"So, this proves…what? Just that she met me at a rally. In public."

Tyson turns back toward the screen and scrolls. "She says you grabbed her ass as this photo was being taken."

"Bullshit."

"I know."

I look over his shoulder, narrowing my eyes to try to see the photo better. "Can you see where my hands are? I always have them at my sides or on people's upper backs for photos."

Tyson squints. "I don't think so. Everyone's standing so close."

I push the home button on his phone, making the image disappear. "Take the day off, Tyson."

"With *this* breaking?"

"Yep. In this line of work, there's always something. You have to learn to just turn it off sometimes."

"I don't know how I can possibly do that," he mutters.

I head for the door to step off the campaign bus. "Go have a tryst, Tyson. It'll do you a world of good."

I walk down the bus stairs into the midmorning sunshine. Despite the shitty press coverage I'm getting right now, I'm feeling good. Chill. Having Reagan here for a few days relaxed me in every way.

A selfish part of me wishes she were still here, but I know she needs to be with her mom right now. Her mom hasn't dated since getting screwed over by her douche ex-husband, Stan Preston. She bought a quiet little beach house, and she says she's happy alone there. Reagan worries about her, though.

I'm too distracted by my hunger to focus on much else, so I walk over to a local diner on the main drag of the small northern Illinois town we're in.

As soon as I walk in, the smells of cooking bacon and syrup make my stomach rumble. The stools at the counter are lined with older men in worn ball caps, and others are holding court at tables in the restaurant.

I lean against the counter until a waitress meets my gaze and asks, "What can I getcha, hon?"

"I'm starving. What do you recommend?"

"The farmer's breakfast is popular. Three strips of bacon, three eggs, two sausage links, and two pieces of toast."

"Perfect. With coffee, please."

"How you want those eggs?"

"Over medium."

"Toast?"

"Wheat, please."

She scrawls the order onto her pad, and I tell her I'll find a seat in a little bit. I can't pass up a chance to meet some voters while I wait.

I gravitate toward a table full of guys waiting on their orders, because one of them is wearing a hat that says "Vietnam Veteran." There's a tug at my heart as I wonder what he saw and did back then.

"Sir?" I approach him as he sits in silence.

"Yeah?"

I offer him my hand to shake. "I just wanted to say thank you for your service."

His brown eyes warm as he shakes my hand. "It was my honor." He eyes the ink on my forearms. "Did you serve?"

"Yes, sir. I'm a Marine."

He nods. "You look familiar, son. But you're not from around here."

"You're running for governor!" One of his friends points at me from across the table. "Against that lady who wants to spend us into the poorhouse."

There's a series of groans and muttered comments around the table. I can't help smiling. Someday, I'll be just like these guys, drinking coffee with my old-timer friends and ruminating on how good things used to be.

"Sit down, Governor," one of the men says, gesturing to an open chair.

"I haven't won yet," I remind them as I sit down on the black vinyl-covered seat.

The veteran waves a hand. "Act like you have. Arrogance is half the battle these days."

"Did you really grab that lady's behind?" one of the guys asks, pronouncing it *bee*-hind. His brows are arched with curiosity.

"Absolutely not."

"Bah." The vet waves his hand again. "Can't believe anything you read in the papers anymore."

The group at the table schools me on the issues they're most concerned about, which I'm not too surprised are Medicare, Social Security, and support for veterans.

Their issues are mostly federal ones, nothing I can have a direct role helping with if elected governor, but it's nice to spend an hour with them anyway. It reminds me why I ran for office in the first place, which was to give people a representative who stayed true to what he ran on and who listened more than he talked.

I leave a nice tip for the waitress, who all the men assured me is a "great gal."

ON THE WALK back to my campaign bus, I take out my phone and see that Reagan texted me two photos. As soon as I click on the first one, my blood starts pumping harder.

It's her at the beach, wearing a purple bikini. She's just ankle-deep in the water, a gorgeous sunset behind her. The second picture is a selfie of her and her mom, both of them smiling radiantly.

Damn, is she gorgeous. It's not just her physical beauty that gets me every single time, but the tenacity, intelligence, and loyalty I see in her deep blue eyes. She's everything I've ever wanted and more.

My only regret is how much she's had to give up to be with me. She's so loyal that I think she sometimes puts me above herself, and I don't feel right about that. If I win the election, I plan to support her fully in whatever comes next for her.

If there's travel, we'll make it work. I love her too much to let her dreams take a back seat to my own.

I feel a renewed sense of purpose. Five years into my

marriage with Reagan, I love her and want her more than I ever have. I wake up every day to make life better for my constituents, but Reagan is the only one I serve. I'd walk through fire for that woman.

As I approach the door to walk onto the bus, though, my good mood is sucked away in an instant as I see who's standing next to the door waiting for me.

My father-in-law.

"Stan." I meet his eyes, but I don't smile. "To what do I owe the pleasure?"

He studies me for a full three seconds, seeming to size up whether I'm being sarcastic or not. I am.

"I think you know damn well why I'm here, Jude." He glares at the closed bus door. "And your driver won't even let me on the bus."

"That's because you're not on the list."

"I'm *family*," he reminds me. This lying bastard is definitely not my favorite relative, but I put up with him for Reagan's sake. "And I offered to show ID since the driver didn't recognize me."

Still arrogant. Even his long fall from grace didn't change that. He hasn't been a senator for several years now, so I'm not surprised my driver Rita didn't recognize him.

"It's not her fault," I point out. "She was following rules, and you're not on the list. Why didn't you call first anyway? What are you doing here?"

He narrows his eyes at me. "Can we talk on the bus?"

I narrow my eyes back. "Yeah, but if it's about something that's gonna upset Reagan, don't expect to stay on there very long."

"Oh, it's something that's *already* upset my daughter."

Rita opens the doors and smiles at me. "Welcome back, Senator."

"Morning, Rita," I pass her the paper cup of coffee I got to-go for her at the diner. "He's with me." I nod at my father-in-law. "So he can get on, this one time."

Stan stalks over to the small booth that serves as a kitchen table and meeting place on the bus. There's a stack of paperwork there, which I sweep aside.

"Afraid I'm out to get you?" Stan quips. "Here to steal all your campaign secrets?"

"What do you want?" I ask him again, ignoring his bait.

"What I *want* is to find out why you're dragging my daughter through a sex scandal. It's time you put her above your political aspirations for once, Jude. Unless the story I read this morning is right and she really has left you."

Rita exits the bus in two seconds flat. She signed nondisclosure agreements and I trust her to be here during any conversation, but it doesn't look like she wants to witness this one. Can't say I blame her. I'd probably punch Stan Preston in his overly active jaw if he weren't Reagan's father.

"Wow." I just stare at him for a few seconds. "I can't believe you of all people are standing here right now saying this to me. I did nothing wrong. You know how dirty politics can get when a race is close. But you actually did betray your family for *decades*."

Stan's face reddens with anger. "That's night and day, Jude. What I did was consensual. I would never dream of touching a woman who didn't want me to."

"Neither would I. And if you think what you did was okay, you're even more of a dirtbag than I already thought you were."

"It wasn't okay. But I've atoned for my mistakes."

"Christ, Stan. Having a secret family isn't a *mistake*. And you only owned up when you got caught."

"Looks like you aren't going to own up at all."

"I didn't do it." My muscles throb with the urge to shove him out the door of my bus. "I know it, and Reagan knows it. That's all that matters."

"Then why is she hiding out at her mother's house? If she wanted to stand by you, wouldn't she be here?" Stan's practically smirking at me.

"Why don't you ask your daughter why she's not here?"

"I've reached out to her."

I scoff. "Yeah, and no response, right? Because you fucked over your family. I *live* for my wife. I'd die before I hurt her."

"Don't you see what you're doing to her? Putting her through this humiliation? Photographers following her all over the place. If you really love her, drop out of the race."

I laugh in a low tone. "Seriously? A spokesman for the Democratic machine is standing here asking me to drop out, but your reasons are strictly altruistic, right?"

"This is only about my daughter."

I point at the bus door. "Get the fuck out of here, Stan. I love your daughter more than life itself, or I'd toss your ass out the door myself. I'll give you three seconds since we're technically related."

He swallows hard and takes a step back. "You wouldn't."

"Try me."

"I said what I needed to say. Reagan may not want me in her life anymore, but I still love her, and I want what's best for her."

"Well, wife of the next governor of our state ain't bad. And I worship the ground that woman walks on. So don't fucking come back, Stan."

He nods once, then says, "You don't want to admit it till your back's against the wall, Jude. I get that. But if the allegations against you aren't true, then why is Dominic Marino trying to buy that woman's silence?"

# REAGAN

My toes sink deep into the mushy wet sand, and water laps at my calves. With my eyes closed, the smell and feel of the beach transport me back to the day Jude and I got married in Hawaii. It will always be one of the happiest days I've ever known.

Life is peaceful here. My mom and I have been walking on the beach several times a day, cooking simple meals, watching movies, and talking a lot.

I feel guilty that it took her upcoming biopsy to get me here. We haven't had time alone like this in years, and I can tell she's loving it as much as I am.

The sunsets here are incredible, and we're soaking tonight's up, walking arm in arm on the stretch of beach that's hers.

"It never gets old," she says, smiling as she looks out

over the vast ocean waves. "I felt like I really started to heal when I moved here. Everything was new, from the smells to the sounds to the views."

"You needed a fresh start."

"I did. And I'm happy here. I'm not ready to leave this world yet, but…if this is my time, I'll go knowing I found peace. When I first found out what your father had done… I didn't think I'd ever be at peace again."

I squeeze her arm. "Do you ever feel lonely here all by yourself?"

"I don't. I read a lot, and I have friends. There's even… a man I've been seeing."

"Mom!" I stop and turn to her, my heart pounding with surprise and happiness. "Why haven't you told me? I've been here for four days, and you're just now mentioning this?"

She tries to hide a smile as she looks out at the crashing waves. "I wasn't trying to keep it from you or anything, I just…we're taking things slow, you know? He lost his wife to ovarian cancer six years ago."

"Slow is good. I'm just so happy you're putting your-self out there again."

"I didn't want to at first, but Ben was persistent. He sent me roses every day until I agreed to have dinner with him."

I swallow against the lump in my throat. This is what

my mom deserves—a man who treasures her. I could cry tears of joy right now.

"Sounds like he knows a good thing when he sees it," I say, bending down to pick up a shell embedded in the sand.

"I haven't told him about the biopsy."

I look up at her. "Why not?"

She shrugs. "The loss of his wife was hard for him. She was very sick. I didn't want to worry him unless I find out it's cancer."

I sigh softly. Even the sound of the word sends a jolt throughout my body. We went to the hospital for her biopsy yesterday, and now we're waiting for the results.

I'm trying to be strong for her, but it's taking everything I've got. I've always loved my mom, but I feel like I've neglected our relationship since getting married.

I've been constantly on the go, always at Jude's side or working on my own career. I haven't taken the time to not just see my mom for holidays but to spend quality time together like we have these past few days.

And now that I see how much I've been missing with her, I want to make it right. I want more one-on-one time with her like this. And if Jude and I have children, I want to bring them to this beach to be with her and have quiet days like this one.

My phone dings with a text, and my mom smiles. "I think Jude's missing you. Give him a call."

"He can wait."

"I owe Ben a call back, actually." She turns toward the house. "Want some tea?"

"I'd love some." I take out my phone and see that she was right—Jude was the one texting me. "I'll be there in a few minutes."

I touch my phone screen to dial Jude, who answers right away.

"Hey, babe, how are you?"

"I'm good."

"Hang on a sec." His voice becomes muffled as he covers the phone and talks to someone else. "Okay, I'm here."

"Tyson?" I ask.

"Yeah. He took almost an entire day off. I'm not sure he'll ever recover."

I laugh at the image of uptight Tyson trying to relax.

"How's campaign life?" I ask.

"Nothing new. I got an unexpected visit from your father, though."

"My father?"

"Yeah. I take it you didn't know he was coming either?"

"No. I haven't talked to him in a while. And I would've let you know if I knew he was coming. He just showed up?"

"Yeah."

"What did he want?"

There's a pause. "Oh, I'm sure you can imagine, given what's going on."

"I can imagine a lot of things he might say. What did he want, Jude?"

Another few moments of silence pass. "I don't think we should talk about it now."

"Why not?"

"I just…I need you to tell me you and I are good. That you're still all in."

"Still all in?" I sit down on a large, flat rock, smoothing my windblown hair away from my face. "Why are you being so cryptic? Tell me what's going on."

He sighs into the phone. "Babe, I can't. We hired a new security team, and the tech guy told me I need to assume none of my communication is secure."

"You mean…someone could be listening?"

"Yeah. Same with our texts. Some conversations are going to have to be in person."

I consider, then say, "Okay. But why are you asking me if things with us are good? I'm just here with—"

"Don't say it. I don't want photographers finding you."

I'm quiet for a few long moments, not sure what it's safe and not safe to say. I've been deliberately avoiding the news, but what am I missing?

Oh God. Are there new accusations against Jude? Is that why he's asking me if we're good? The thought makes my stomach roll nervously.

Until I know, I have to assume things are the same. "Of course we're good. I love you."

"I love you too. And I miss you. I'm thinking of you guys, babe. Both of you."

"I know. Thank you."

"Any idea when you'll know?"

"Should be in a couple days."

"Okay." His voice sounds weary. "I'm sorry, babe, but I have to go. Tyson's about to have a coronary. We're on our way to a meeting."

"I understand."

"I'll call you tonight, when I'm all done."

"Okay. Bye, babe."

"Bye. Love you."

I walk alone on the beach for a few minutes, giving my mom time to talk to Ben and also thinking about what my father could have possibly said to Jude.

He's got no business coming near either one of us. I tolerate him, but that's about it.

Some hurt just runs too deep.

# JUDE

By the time Dominic Marino bothers to call me back—two days after I left him a message—I'm out of patience.

"What can I do for you, Senator Titan?" he asks when I pick up the call.

"I think a better question is, what have you already tried to do for me without my permission?"

There are a couple seconds of silence on the other end of the line.

"I'm sure I misheard you," Dominic finally says. "Because if I *were* doing your dirty work—not that I'm saying I am—you'd be thanking me for it."

I look up at the ceiling and then step off the campaign bus. I don't want anyone—even my trusted staffers—hearing this conversation.

When I'm a safe distance away, alone in the middle of a parking lot, I respond. "I took one meeting with you. And in that meeting, I asked you for nothing."

"But I offered my support," Dominic says in a cool tone. "Which you said you'd be grateful for."

"Support means voting for me. Telling others about my platform. Maybe contributing. It doesn't make you a spokesman for me. What have you done?"

"You have a problem. I'm making it go away. The less you know about it, the better."

Dammit. Reagan was right about Dominic Marino. I should have known. Guys like him try to buy politicians' allegiance in crooked ways like this. It's everything I refuse to be a part of in politics.

"Listen to me, Marino." My voice is smooth and sure. "Any offer you've made to anyone needs to be taken off the table. Not only will I never be your pawn, I'm about to put your name at the top of my shit list."

"Are you threatening me, Senator?" He sounds amused.

"Not at all. What I'm saying is that if you want a friend in the governor's mansion, you're talking to the wrong candidate. I don't want anything to do with you."

"I see. Not even if Miss Culbertson is eager to accept…a gift from me in exchange for a full retraction?"

"No. Keep your money. I'm not interested in having anything to do with you."

I end the call and shove my phone into my pocket, putting my hands on my head. The race between my opponent and me is tight, because she's pouring millions of her own money into her campaign. I've had to ramp up time spent campaigning, and there's no time left for working out or even a quick morning run.

I'm going to have to build that time back in. With Reagan gone, I have to find another way to relieve stress.

My favorite way to release tension is a couple hours of sweaty sex with her. But until she gets back from Florida, I have to rely on my hand, which isn't even a close second to my wife's body.

Her mouth. Her toned legs. Her breathy voice. God, I miss her. I want to talk to her about this shit with Marino, but I can't because of the secure phone line issue.

There's no one else in the world I can just let my guard completely down with. And I know her, she wouldn't say I told you so. She'd tell me Marino's a dick and everything was going to be okay.

It will be okay. I believe that. But the road's getting rocky, and I don't want to cross the finish line without my wife by my side. Win or lose, I need her with me.

My phone buzzes in my pocket, and I take it out. It's a calendar reminder that I have a meeting with my new communications strategist in five minutes.

Fuck. I don't get why my strategy can't be "Tell the truth and work your hardest." Politics can get convoluted.

But the RNC is completely behind me, and I appreciate the resources they've sent.

This woman, Vanessa Grayson, is supposed to be the best. She's run focus groups, spent time with my pollsters and Tyson, and even took the interns out for lunch one day. Her research into messaging has been thorough, and I need to listen to what she has to say.

By the time I get back to the bus, there's no one left on it but Vanessa. Even Rita's seat at the front of the bus is empty.

"Tyson took everyone to the pub down the street for lunch," Vanessa says. "He said you can text him if you want him to bring back food for you."

I slide into the other side of the kitchen booth from her, setting my phone down on the table.

"Okay." I arch my brows. "You ready to get started?"

"I think I'll grab a drink first. Do you want anything?"

I shake my head and look down at the stack of papers on the table in front of me.

"These demographics are a little surprising," I say, scanning a chart.

"How so?"

I look over and see that she just took a bottle of water from the refrigerator and she's closing it.

"I thought I'd poll with more likely votes from college-educated women," I say.

"Yeah, your opponent is a self-made female million-aire, so she's got that demographic locked up."

Vanessa unscrews the cap from her water and takes a sip, then sets the bottle down on the counter. She reaches for the top button of her red blouse and unbuttons it.

"It's hot in here, don't you think?" She runs a fingertip down the line between her breasts, now exposed thanks to the button she undid.

Fuck. I don't need this right now. Alone on my bus with a woman, while false allegations about another woman and me are still swirling? I'm kicking Tyson's ass for putting me in this position.

"You know, it is hot," I lie, standing up. "I could really go for a cold beer. I'm gonna run down to that pub and get lunch with the others."

"What?" Vanessa furrows her brow. "But what about our meeting?"

I hold up the stack of papers she left on the table. "I think I need to go over all this first. Then Tyson and I will sit down with you."

"I'm going to go over it with you now. Tyson doesn't need to be here."

She takes a step closer to me, flicking her long blond hair over her shoulder. I give her a tight smile.

"You know, I'm late calling my wife back. I'm gonna call her on the way to the pub. Can we bring anything back for you?"

"No, I'm fine, but—"

I turn and leave, not letting her finish. I'm not taking any chances. If she tries to get with me and I turn her down, which I would, she could get pissed and say it was me who hit on her.

From Dominic Marino to my own coms strategist, I'm having to keep it from looking like I'm in bed with people I'm not. I don't have time for this shit. Legitimate campaigning is hard enough.

I make it to the pub in five minutes, and Tyson gives me a confused look as soon as he sees me.

"Outside. Now." I scowl at him, and he drops a French fry in midair.

"What's going on?" he asks in a low tone from the alley behind the pub.

"Don't ever leave me alone with a woman again unless it's my wife."

Tyson's eyes widen. "Oh. You mean…shit."

"It's fine this time, I got out of it, but it can't happen again."

"No, you're right. I didn't even think of that because she's on our team, but…yeah, you're right."

"You need to be like a pimple on my ass until election night," I say. "We even need to be sharing a hotel room unless I'm with Reagan."

"Yeah, okay. I'm not spooning you, though." Tyson laughs weakly.

"No, you're sure as fuck not. Now let's get in there, and you can buy me lunch to make it up to me."

He rolls his eyes. "When are *you* gonna buy *me* lunch?"

"Tyson, if we win this, I'll buy you a steak dinner."

He muses, then nods. "I like steak."

"And I like winning. So let's figure out how to make us both happy."

"Guess I need to sit in on the coms strategy meeting, huh?"

"Yeah. And every other meeting with her."

He nods. "It's kinda bullshit that hot chicks are only into you when you're married, and I'm single."

"You want her, go after her," I tell him.

Tyson flushes a dark crimson. "I couldn't…I mean…"

"Let's go eat, man." I clap him on the back. "You don't have time for dating anyway."

"True," he grumbles. "I'd be happy with a shower right now."

"As long as you don't leave me alone with you know who to take one."

"You mean…Voldemort?" He snorts at his attempt at a joke.

I remember the offended look on Vanessa's face as I left the bus and decide that's not a bad name for her at all. The stakes have gotten so high that most anyone could become the villain.

# REAGAN

I'M WALKING INTO MY MOM'S KITCHEN TO POUR ANOTHER cup of coffee when I see the tears streaming down her face.

I stop breathing as I look at her. I can practically hear Jude speaking to me, his voice deep and even.

*Be strong, Reagan. Be strong. Come what may, she needs you to be the strong one.*

"What is it?" I ask her.

"I just got off the phone. My results came in, and…I'm okay." She chokes out a sob. "It's benign."

I let out the breath I feel like I've been holding for nearly two weeks now, breaking into tears at the same time. She stands up, and we wrap our arms around each other.

The relief flows through my entire body. It's physical, emotional—spiritual.

After a minute, my mom pulls away to grab a couple tissues. She passes me one, and I mop the tears from my cheeks.

"I need to call your sister," she says, her shoulders dropping with relief. "And Ben."

"Did you tell him?"

She shakes her head. "No, but I'm going to tell him everything now."

"Do I get to meet him? I'd love to meet him while I'm here."

She considers. "We could do that. I figured you'd want to get right back on the campaign trail."

"I want to stay a little while longer. I'm really enjoying this time with you. And now we have something to celebrate."

She takes a deep breath and blows it out. "Yes, we do. Oh, I'm so relieved, Reagan."

She squeezes my hand, then picks up her phone and walks out onto her deck. I head to the guest room I'm staying in and grab my own phone, typing out a text to Jude.

**Me: We got good news. All clear.**

He responds right away.

**Jude: Babe, that's great. You must be relieved.**

**Me: I can't even put into words how relieved I am.**

**Jude: Missing you bad. Can't wait to have you back with me.**

**Me: About that…**

**Jude: Yeah?**

**Me: I want to stay and spend some more time with my mom. It's been a long time since I've had time alone with her.**

**Jude: Sure, I understand.**

**Me: So just coded texts and phone calls for a little longer. ☹**

**Jude: You're worth the wait. Sorry, I've gtg. In an editorial board meeting.**

**Me: Knock 'em dead, Titan. I love you.**

**Jude: Love you too.**

I put my phone down and relax into an armchair. This whole thing with my mom has really put things into perspective for me. For too long, I've been focused on poll numbers, campaign contributions, and political platforms. Jude and I both have.

We remind ourselves that we're lucky to be here—in positions that allow us to truly change people's lives. But it's a grind, and what we don't acknowledge often enough is the cost to our personal lives.

I need to clear my mind. I take a long, hot shower and pull my wet hair into a bun. The beach life is nice and low maintenance. No blow-dryers needed here.

Then I tell my mom I'm taking her out for lunch and some shopping today. We hit a local seafood place, and then she shows me all her favorite little boutique stores.

I buy way more than I should since I do have to fly back home eventually, but today I've decided to be impractical. I'm not going to hurry, stress, or worry. When we stop for ice cream at the end of our day, I only think about what sounds good, not why I shouldn't be eating any of it.

"How are Kennedy and Chris doing?" my mom asks as we sit on a bench at the beach eating our ice cream.

I swipe a melting stream of chocolate ice cream from my rocky road cone. "I haven't talked to Chris in a while. Kennedy's really good. She and Nix took a month off to go on a big diving trip near the Philippines."

"Wow. Diving?"

I nod. My mom accepted Chris and Kennedy, my father's children from his longtime affair, without question. She knows none of what happened is their fault. Kennedy still struggles with the truth of it all. She didn't know my father had another family either.

"Finding out about my brother and another sister was the only good that came out of all that," I say, half to myself.

"I don't know about that."

I turn to face my mom. "What do you mean?"

"I'm happier now than I was then."

"You always seemed happy to me growing up."

"I wasn't *un*happy. I had my kids, and I felt like I was doing something noble by being the wife of a senator. Supporting the greater good or something."

"You couldn't have known what was going on, Mom."

She looks out at a boat passing by. "I don't mean all of that. I've had a lot of time to think about it, and in retrospect, even if your father had been who I thought he was, it wouldn't have been worth it."

"How so?"

She starts to speak but hesitates, then shakes her head. "I don't think we should go there. You're in the thick of Jude's campaign for governor. You don't need to hear my thoughts on this right now."

I arch my brows with curiosity. "I want to hear your thoughts on it, though."

She sighs softly. "It wasn't worth it. Sometimes I ask myself if all the time your father and I were apart was part of the reason he strayed."

"Mom." I shake my head. "You can't think that way. He was wrong. So wrong. There's no excuse for it."

"I know." She nods in agreement. "I really do. But what I'm saying is…our relationship was never…magic, you know? It was always about how far he could go in office and what things looked like to the outside world. We lived for appearances. If I could do it over again, I'd do it so differently."

"How so?"

"I'd marry a man for whom a life with me and our children was enough." She sits back against the bench. "A man who didn't want to be powerful or influential.

Who wanted to coach little league and go to ballet recitals."

I think back to all the times my mom sat alone in the stands at my sporting events. The parent-teacher conferences she attended by herself. The dinners where there was an empty seat at the table.

We were often on the go. That was our life, just like my life is now.

"Tell me about Ben," I say, trying not to think about how deeply her words are impacting me.

"Oh." Her cheeks turn pink as she smiles. "He's a retired physics professor. He loves sailing and cooking."

"Sailing? Have you been sailing with him?"

"A few times."

I nudge her and laugh. "I can't believe you've been holding out on me. A physics professor who sails? Does he have his own sailboat?"

"He does. He was born into a wealthy family, but teaching has always been his passion."

"And do you feel…magic with him?"

She wraps her arms around herself, and a grin spreads across her face, lighting her up. "I do. For the first time in my life, just being together is enough. When he looks at me, I feel like there's nothing more in the world he wants at that moment. And I feel the same way about him."

I fight back happy tears. "Mom, I'm so thrilled for you. You deserve that kind of love and happiness."

Her smile softens. "So do you, Reagan. You know I adore Jude, but sometimes I wonder if the two of you are paying the same price I did. Giving up too much of yourselves in the name of public service."

I look down at my lap. It's like she can read my mind. I've been having the same thoughts lately.

"I don't mean to overstep." She puts her hand over mine. "I just want you guys to stop and smell the roses, so to speak. I want you to do better than I did."

"I know, Mom. I'm feeling it too. There's this constant feeling that we aren't doing enough. That we need to get up earlier to start campaigning, stay out later, add one more event…"

"It never ends." She shakes her head. "Even after your father won his Senate seat, the campaigning never ended because he had to *keep* it. And if Jude becomes governor…that's an even bigger stage. With more pressure. Seeing the stories in the news about this woman accusing him of harassment…" She sighs heavily. "It's been hard for me, Reagan. I never want you to go through what I did."

"But Jude didn't touch that woman. I know him."

"I don't believe for a second that he did. But there'll be more accusations, and then there are the people trying to buy him off. It never ends."

I nod, closing my eyes and breathing in the ocean air. "I thought that if it wasn't me holding office—if it was

Jude, whom I believe in with everything I am—that it would be easier."

"It's hard to see someone you love dragged through false accusations. Worked into the ground."

"It is. But I love him. And public service is where his heart is."

My mom's eyes flood with emotion. "Just don't forget that it matters where your heart lies, too. It matters every bit as much."

She puts her arm around me, and I lean into her. It's been a long time since I considered what I really want. I'm part of a "we" instead of a "me" now, and Jude is my whole world.

But if he's my world, don't I have a right to want more of him than I'm getting? To not want to share him with so many people?

Passionate nights together have become a stolen luxury, but why? I need to find a way to talk to my husband, but there's a major communications barrier thanks to his security team.

I want to tell Jude it's not that I want more, but that I want less. Less of everything that isn't just him and me. My mom's cancer scare and our conversation today reminded me that life can be short.

I never want to look back and wish we'd set aside career goals to focus on the only thing that truly matters—us.

# JUDE

"JUDE, DID YOUR WIFE LEAVE YOU BECAUSE OF THE accusations against you?"

A reporter jams a microphone in my face, and I silently glare at him. His eyes widen as I stare him down.

"I'm late to a meeting with constituents." I put my hand on the microphone and ease it away from my face. "Excuse me."

"Jessica Culbertson says you tried to pay her off so she'd rescind her allegations against you. Is that true?"

I stop walking, conscious of the cameras filming me. My instinct is to tell this guy to fuck off, but I can't.

"No, it's not true. Beyond the photo taken at a rally with Miss Culbertson that's been circulating, I've never seen or spoken to her."

"The photo where you touched her inappropriately?" A female reporter arches her brows at me in challenge.

"I did no such thing."

"What does your wife think about the new photos showing you in a hotel room with another woman?"

I hide my amusement at the continuing assumption that it's another woman in those photos. "My wife and I are good. I'll let her know you guys are concerned about her, though."

"Is it true you're getting advice from your father-in-law, Stan Preston?" a reporter I can't see barks out.

"Guys." Tyson intervenes, putting an arm out to hold back the reporters. "He's late for a meeting with constituents. Let him through."

My meeting is with a group of environmentalists. When I walk into the room, several are already fired up.

"I'll vote for Big Bird before this guy," I hear a guy mutter to someone next to him as I walk by.

So, it's not exactly a friendly crowd. But that's okay. I represent everyone in the state of Illinois, and that means I'll never stop listening to them.

"Thanks for coming, guys." I slide into place behind the lectern and take the bottle of water Tyson passes me. "I figured we could just go right into questions."

"Why was the media barred from this meeting?" a woman demands from the front row.

"Because all their questions are about my personal life,

not the environment. Your concerns would get drowned out."

She shakes her head. "If there's no one recording what you say, you can promise us anything, and no one will ever know you said it."

Several people in the crowd nod.

"Look, you guys have known me for more than six years now. I think I've proven to be a man of my word. I'm not gonna tell you what you want to hear. Mostly, I came here today to listen. But if you want to record this meeting, I have no problem with that. I just don't want reporters in here yelling out questions that have nothing to do with what your group is about."

The woman takes out her cell phone and points it at me, apparently deciding to record.

It's gonna be a long day on the campaign trail.

---

I SPEND my fifteen-minute afternoon break in a small bunk on the campaign bus, the curtain closed around me as I text with Reagan.

**Me: This would be the perfect time for some stress relief. I'm just sayin'…**

She sends back a laughing emoji. What the fuck? Am I the only one dying from lack of sex? I type out another message.

**Me: Any idea when you'll be back?**

**Reagan: Not yet.**

My skin tingles with the same awareness I used to feel in combat situations. Something's not right. But I can't come out and say that, because if our conversation is being monitored, something could be misconstrued and used against me.

But I have to say something.

**Me: You doing okay, babe?**

**Reagan: I'm great. Getting a tan and learning to cook some of my mom's favorite recipes. How about you? Busy?**

She's campaigned before, and she has access to my schedule. She has to know I'm working my ass off. And I selfishly wish she wanted to be here with me.

**Me: Yeah, very busy.**

**Reagan: How are the new staffers working out?**

**Me: Pretty good overall.**

**Reagan: You seem distant. Is everything okay?**

*I* seem distant? She's the one working on her tan in Florida and not seeming to miss me at all while I'm lying in a hot, coffin-sized bunk with a raging boner.

I try to cool my resentment. Reagan deserves a break, and she doesn't spend enough time with her mom.

**Me: I'm okay. Just tired. And missing you.**

**Reagan: I miss you too. There's so much I want to**

talk to you about. I've had a lot of time for thinking about things here.

Me: Such as?

Reagan: Nothing I can say right now.

Fuck. I've had it with not being able to have a real conversation with my wife. Not to mention my frustration over not being able to touch her or even lay eyes on her.

I'm fighting hard in this race, because I want her sacrifices for me to be worth it. I want her to be proud of me. But I don't want to do it alone.

Before I proposed to Reagan, I thought long and hard about spending the rest of my life with her. Would I grow restless? Would I miss the freedom of the unmarried life?

I decided she was worth taking the leap for. Since the moment I laid eyes on her, she's been the only one for me. And surprisingly, marriage suited me well from the beginning. I've never felt restless or in need of space.

Quite the opposite, actually. I don't just want my wife with me, I need her. Even if that does make me a selfish asshole. She grounds me and is the only one I can completely let go in front of.

I type out the words I can't hold on to anymore.

Me: I need to see you.

Reagan: Is everything okay?

Me: Things are fine, but I need to see you. I'll fly down there if you don't want to come here.

Reagan: It's not that I don't want to see you, babe.

You know that, right? I'm just trying to get in some quality time with my mom.

**Me: I know. But can you spare one night for me?**

**Reagan: Sarcastic much?**

**Me: Reagan. When and where? I need a night with my wife.**

**Reagan: Okay. Let me ask my mom what her plans are.**

My dick is straining uncomfortably against my fly as I stare at the beige ceiling of the bus. I hate this feeling of not being in control. But my hand isn't gonna cut it anymore. I need to fuck my wife.

The three dots that signify she's writing a text appear on the screen, and I stare at them as I wait.

**Reagan: Saturday night. I can fly home to Chicago. Can you swing a night at our place?**

**Me: Yes.**

**Reagan: Okay, I'll text my itinerary so you can pick me up if possible.**

My aggravation grows as I keep reading her messages, which sound the same as what she'd send to any lesser-known acquaintance. My balls look like a fucking Smurf, and she's cool as a cucumber.

I fire off a hotheaded message.

**Me: Thanks for the favor. Looking forward to seeing you too.**

**Reagan: What's that supposed to mean?**

Me: You could at least act like you're excited to see me. It's been almost two weeks.

Reagan: Of course, I'm excited to see you. We're married, though. I didn't think I had to say that every time I'm going to see you.

Me: What, married people don't excite each other anymore?

Reagan: Jude, you're being ridiculous.

Me: And you're being indifferent.

Reagan: You're just looking for a fight.

Me: No, I'm looking for my wife to give a shit that she hasn't seen me in two weeks.

Reagan: You know why I needed to be here. And you're busy with the campaign.

Me: Which I thought you wanted to be part of.

Reagan: I have been part of it. But I'll be damned if I'll stand there looking starry-eyed every time you speak just so photographers can take pics of me "standing by my man."

Me: Yeah, God forbid.

Reagan: You're pissing me off.

Me: I have to go. I've got a thing in 5 min.

Reagan: Great timing. Sweep in, be a dick, and then sweep out.

Me: Check my fucking schedule if you think I'm lying.

Reagan: I'll talk to you later.

**Me: Thanks for working me into your busy tanning schedule.**

**Reagan: Fuck you, Jude.**

I toss my phone onto the thin, lumpy mattress and blow out a breath. I was being a dick, I admit it. But I can only take so much.

She's in Florida, apparently not missing me much, and "thinking about things." I need to lay eyes on her and see that's she's still mine in every way.

Just like I know I married a stubborn hard-ass of a woman, she knows she married a brooding hard ass of a man.

When I push the curtain aside on the bunk and slide out, I look over and see Tyson and Vanessa sitting at the table.

Christ. I know I was only texting with Reagan and not talking, but I feel invaded as Vanessa eye-fucks me.

Campaign life is a grind. The one person I want close is too far away, and everyone else is constantly up my ass.

---

Somehow, Vanessa's managing to appear focused on the strategies she's reviewing with Tyson and me, but I'm pretty sure it's her toes tracing along my calf under the table and not Tyson's.

"Uh..." I clear my throat and move my leg away. "This

looks good except I don't know about moving criticism of the budget to the top of my messaging. Shouldn't we stay positive with our main talking points?"

"This is polling as the issue voters are most concerned about," Vanessa says. "And we can mix in some positive with the negative by talking about fiscal responsibility."

I nod. "Okay. Tyson, can we adjust my stump speech before the next stop?"

"Yeah, we've got time."

I return to reading the charts in front of me. Within a couple seconds, Vanessa's bare foot is tracing its way back up my leg.

"Tyson, can you see if there's a place nearby to get some highlighters?" she asks. "I meant to pick some up earlier, but I ran out of time."

"Uh…" He looks at me, knowing I don't want him to leave.

Vanessa looks back and forth between us. "What? Am I missing something?"

"We'll be fine without highlighters," I say. "Let's finish up."

"I don't see why it's such a big—"

I cut her off. "Look, Vanessa. I'm not willing to be left alone with you."

She furrows her brow. "Are you serious?"

I rub my temple. "Yeah. First of all, get your foot off my leg."

Her cheeks redden as she slips her foot away.

"Second of all, I'm a happily married man. If you're gonna work on my campaign, keep your hands and feet and whatever else to yourself. Understood?"

Vanessa's face flushes an even deeper shade of crimson. "I think you misunderstood, Jude."

"Were you thinking that was Tyson's leg, then?"

She looks away. "I came here to *help*. I didn't need this job. I have plenty of others who will hire me in a second."

"Leave, then." I shrug and push away the stack of papers.

"Is that really what you want?"

Tyson speaks up. "I think it's for the best that you go. We'll pay you the full amount agreed to."

Vanessa huffs before sliding out of the booth and leaving without another word. As soon as she's gone, Tyson and I just look at each other for a few seconds.

"I'm taking Saturday and Sunday off," I say.

He rolls his eyes. "Perfect. We just lost our strategist, the election's less than a month away, and you're taking the weekend off."

"Yep." I get up and take a bottle of water from the fridge. "Ready to rewrite my speech?"

Tyson's weary sigh is my only answer.

23

# REAGAN

As soon as I walk in my front door, it hits me how much I've missed home. I breathe in the fresh scent of wood from the recent refinishing of the floors on our main level.

Much as I'd like to curl up on the couch and relax, I need to get ready for Jude's arrival later. I took an early flight, and he can't get here until early evening. That gives me a couple hours to get my hair blown out and have all my overgrown areas waxed.

Tonight will be a reminder of what I wish we could have all the time. Part of me wants to talk to Jude about my feelings, but I'm not ready yet. He's in the thick of campaigning, and I don't want to upset him. Besides, I'm pretty sure he'll have other things in mind when he gets here.

Our text fighting won't lessen his sexual appetite for me. If anything, it'll heighten his desire to put me in my place the only way he can.

Just the thought makes my knees weaken slightly. None of the men I was with before Jude hold a candle to him in the bedroom. He's like a drug I can never get enough of.

I manage not only a trip to my salon but also a stop at a lingerie store for a sheer red bra and panties that lace up in back with a ribbon. I smile as I slip on yoga pants with a hole in one knee and an old campaign shirt of mine from when I was a state rep with a stain on front.

I'm going to have some fun with Jude tonight. In more than one way.

"Hey," he calls out from the front entrance. "You here, babe?"

"Hi, yeah." I greet him as I jog down the stairs.

I get to the living room, and we just look at each other from about ten feet apart for a few seconds, both of us sizing up whether we're still mad at each other.

Finally, I see Jude move in my direction, and I move toward him at the same time. We meet, and he wraps me in his arms.

I close my eyes and bury my face in his neck as he holds me. God, I've missed him. The faint, sporty scent of his body wash smells as much like home to me as our newly sanded floors.

"Apology accepted," I murmur.

He grunts in response and pulls back a little, smoothing a few strands of dark hair away from my face before kissing me.

"I missed my gorgeous, stubborn, cantankerous wife," he says against my lips.

My single note of laughter is amused. "And I missed my sexy, moody, horse's ass husband."

"Horse's ass?" His tone is offended, but his eyes are lit with amusement.

"That's what I said."

He tightens his hold on my waist and pulls me against him hard, kissing me again.

"Keep running that mouth, Mrs. Titan. You'll be using it for other things later."

"About that…" I look away, pretending to be uncomfortable.

"What?" Jude lowers his brows in a serious look.

"You know…it's that time of the month, and my period is awful. I've got cramps and a headache. I was thinking we could just order in some food, cuddle, and get a great night of sleep? Maybe watch a movie? I already put on my comfy clothes."

Jude's face freezes in an expression that's half horrified, half nauseated. If I didn't have to play along, I'd burst out laughing.

"Are you fucking serious?" He shakes his head slightly.

"What? You just wanted me to spread my legs? Don't you want to talk? We haven't talked in forever."

"Yeah, but…" He runs a hand through his dark, slightly rumpled hair. "I was hoping for both."

I shrug. "Sorry, babe."

"Okay." He looks up at the ceiling, exasperated, and it's all I can do not to fall down laughing.

His erection softens slightly against my thigh. Poor Jude.

"We fired the new strategy person," he says, taking my hand and leading me to sit down next to him on the couch.

"Why?"

"She was being unprofessional toward me."

I furrow my brow and curl my legs up beneath me. "You mean mouthy, or…"

He shakes his head. "I'm pretty sure she wanted to get with me. Tyson fired her a second before I was about to."

"Okay."

I run my fingertips over his forehead, down his temple, to his stubbled jawline. He closes his eyes and rests a hand on my thigh.

"I've really missed you," he says.

"I've really missed you, too. I wish you could be down at my mom's with me. It's so peaceful there."

"Maybe I can come down soon. I need to see that purple bikini in person."

I smile and kiss him softly. He leans his head back against the couch, eyes still closed. When I look at his lap and see that his erection is tenting his khakis, I decide I've tormented him long enough.

"Hey, babe?" I say, standing up and grabbing the bottom of my shirt.

"Hmm?" He lifts up his head and looks at me.

I pull the shirt off over my head and toss it to the floor, revealing my red bra with lace cups.

"I was kidding about my period. And the headache. And also the cuddling."

Realization dawns on his face, and he shoots up from the couch, catching me around the waist. I squeal as he picks me up and throws me over his shoulder.

"Not another word, Mrs. Titan. Not one more word from that smart mouth."

"Jude!" I shriek, laughing and trying to push the hair out of my face.

"That was a word," he says gruffly, smacking my ass so hard I cry out and jump.

"Mango," I say playfully. That gets me another hard smack.

"Apple." The next smack is so hard it stings. And I like it.

"Carnivorous," I say softly, bracing myself.

Jude spanks my ass as he runs up the stairs, not stopping until he dumps me on the bed. He immediately grabs the waistband of my yoga pants and jerks them off in one second flat.

My body warms under his hungry gaze. As he unfastens his belt buckle, I get on my knees and turn around, showing him the back of my panties.

"You like?" I shake my booty a little, and he groans with approval.

"Fuck, babe. That's hot."

I reach for the ribbon at the small of my back. "Want me to untie it?"

"Don't you dare."

His pants drop to the floor with a thudding sound.

"No ropes tonight," he says in a low tone. "Tonight, you're gonna be as still and silent as I tell you to, because if you don't, I'll stop whatever I'm doing."

I give him a sultry smile over my shoulder. "I'll try."

"I mean it. This is the only place I get to own that sassy mouth of yours. Comply, and you get to come. Or…you can try to be a better girl in the morning."

I moan softly, my skin hot and my core achy. My body has never responded to anyone or anything the way it does to Jude. I've been conditioned by his deep, sexy voice and hard, unyielding body. My husband is *not* all talk.

Once his clothes are off, he walks over to the bed and stands at its side, grabbing my hips to move me so I'm kneeling on the bed in front of him, facing away from him and leaving my ass at his mercy.

I'm expecting a good, hard spanking. My skin tingles in anticipation of it. Instead, he brushes his fingers across my skin gently.

The unexpected lightness of it sends a shiver down my spine. He slowly caresses every inch of me, reacquainting himself with my body.

When he gathers my hair into his fist and tugs me into an upright position, I gasp and moan simultaneously.

Putting a knee on the mattress, he leans in and kisses the back of my neck, his hand still wrapped around my hair. He pulls my head back and kisses my shoulder, nipping at my skin until I whimper.

"Not another sound," he whispers in my ear, "until I give you permission to make one."

I exhale deeply as his free hand glides down my bare stomach, his fingers dipping into the waistband of my panties.

"Mmm…missed me, didn't you, babe?"

He slides his fingers across my wet clit, groaning. His warm breath against my neck makes me pant as I force myself not to moan or cry out.

My back arches as his fingers move in and out of me, nearly sending me over the edge every time they circle my clit. He stops after just a few seconds every time, though, leaving me breathing heavy and silently begging for more.

Every nerve ending in my body is firing as he takes me to the brink and back over and over. I don't even consider begging for release, because I know he means what he says about stopping.

This is the one place I love ceding control; he's the only person I've ever wanted to cede it to.

"You want a nice hard fuck?" he asks, tugging on the ribbon at the back of my panties. "Just tell me if you do."

He's playing with me. If I say yes, he'll stop. But *damn*, is it hard to stay silent right now. I bite my lip and force myself not to speak.

Jude makes a low sound of amusement as he unties the ribbon and slides the panties down my thighs.

My skin buzzes with arousal and the hot anticipation of his next move. More spanking? My ass cheeks are still burning from before, but I'm hoping he's not done.

It's the not knowing that nearly undoes me when we're in bed together and he's in full control. I never know what his next move will be, but I know I'll give in to whatever deliciously sweet torture he wants.

I feel him moving behind me, and I gasp with surprise when he gets on his back and slides his head between my legs. He gives me a devilish wink as I look down at him.

"Fuck my face, baby," he says, grabbing my ass and squeezing it until I groan. "Show me how bad you want to come."

*Oh God.*

I love it when he does this. I don't deserve this man whose repayment for my teasing is an earth-shattering orgasm. I don't say so, though. Instead, I sink onto his mouth, my lips parting with pleasure as his warm tongue slides over me.

This always leads to a fast, hard orgasm. I circle my hips, the sensation building steadily. I'm panting as I grab the headboard and hold on, riding him as he tongue-fucks me and sucks on my clit.

I come undone in the most exquisite way, tears burning my eyes as I cry out his name, and his fingertips sink into my ass cheeks.

It's all I can do to tumble off of him and lie back. He gives me a sexy grin, his face gleaming with my juices.

"I hope you're about to fuck me," I say breathlessly.

"Thought I'd let you recover a minute first."

"Now," I say softly. "Please."

He gets to his knees and pushes my thighs back, groaning hard as he thrusts all the way inside me. It's pure heaven, watching his expression of bliss as he pumps himself in and out of my soaked, satisfied pussy.

When he starts to slow down, knowing it'll take me longer to come the second time, I shake my head. "Don't stop, baby. Give me everything. I want it right now."

His expression twists with pleasure as he continues, holding on to my legs as he plows into me again and again. Nothing compares to the feeling of having him buried deep inside me, my body promising him a powerful release.

When his already dark eyes turn into coal, I know he's seconds away. He locks his gaze with mine and groans loudly with his final deep thrust, holding himself inside me as he comes.

The tension and worry are erased from his face as he exhales deeply and leans down to kiss me. Only I get to do that to this beautiful man. I may cause some of his moods, but I can also cure them like no one else.

I cradle his cheeks in my hand and kiss him gently. It's moments like this when the depth of my love for him almost scares me. It's an abyss I can't control my fall into.

He's worth the fall, though. For him, I'd fall ten thousand times. It'll be hard to return to my mom's tomorrow, but I still feel like that's where I'm supposed to be right now.

# 24

## JUDE

I TURN UP THE VOLUME ON THE BOB MARLEY SONG playing on my Yukon's stereo. Life is good, and not just because I'm driving myself around in my own vehicle for the first time in a while.

I've had my phone powered down since right before I walked in the door to see Reagan yesterday. We both remained cut off from the rest of the world until I dropped her off at the airport an hour ago.

I hated to say goodbye to her again, but our time together rejuvenated me. It reminded me that we're just apart temporarily, and I only have to keep campaigning for another two weeks.

Win or lose, I'm ready to move on with my life. I need more time with Reagan. I also need more moments like this one, where I can breathe and think and be by myself.

Having a driver is practical when I'm campaigning, and if I win the election, I suppose I'll have one all the time. But driving my own car and listening to my own music isn't something I'm willing to give up completely.

Reagan and I have talked about driving the coast of California in a convertible, not making any plans and just stopping where and when we feel the urge. I'm ready to take that trip with her.

The rally I'm attending is in Winnetka, and I deliberately park at the back of the conference center's parking lot to give myself a few extra minutes of alone time.

I'm approaching the building's entrance when Tyson comes rushing up to me. His hair is going in a hundred directions, which means he's been running his hands through it like he does when he's nervous.

"Where have you been?" He throws his arms out at his sides, eyes wide with judgment.

"I told you I was taking time off," I remind him.

"Yeah, but you haven't even been responding to texts."

I shrug. "Because I was *off*, man. Completely off. But I'm back now. What's up?"

He leans in to speak by my ear.

"Don't show any reaction to what I'm about to say. The photographers are watching, and I know they want to get a shot of you reacting, so don't do it."

I nod and he continues.

"Jessica Culbertson's rep called me. They're holding a

news conference in an hour to announce that she was paid off by a radical left-wing supporter to make up the story about you. She feels guilt now and wants to give the money back."

"Guilt?" I murmur skeptically.

"This is basically her begging us not to sue her."

I nod again and turn to speak into Tyson's ear. "At least it's before the election. This should give us a boost."

"Yeah, I expect it will. I've already drafted a response for you."

He passes me a paper, and I read it. It's diplomatic, thanking Miss Culbertson for doing the right thing and urging my opponent to focus on the issues that matter to voters.

My face is impassive as I pass it back to Tyson. "Looks good. Thanks, man."

"Let's not leak this." He gives me a serious look. "Don't even hint at it in your remarks."

"I'll stick to this script, don't worry."

"And Jude—be careful. No shit-eating grins about anything whatsoever. The photographers can turn that around on us."

"Got it."

He puts a hand on my shoulder. "You ready to go in?"

I take my phone out of my pocket and turn it on. "Hang on. I need to let my wife know."

"Don't. It may not be secure."

I shake my head. "I don't care. If the news conference is in an hour, no one can do anything with this anyway. I have to let Reagan know."

As my phone comes to life, messages from Tyson start popping up on my screen.

"Christ, man. Forty-one texts?" I scowl at him.

"You weren't responding."

"I don't get how sending more texts would make anyone respond."

I type out a message to Reagan: **Good news, babe. The truth about the allegations against me will be coming out in an hour.**

Her plane is in the air right now, but I want her to see this message as soon as she turns her phone back on.

I'm beyond relieved. Whether or not I become the next governor of my state, the truth is being told. My integrity means more to me than any elected office.

I'm on point for the rally and all my other stops of the day. Between my night with Reagan and the bombshell news conference that the allegations against me are false, I'm back at the top of my game.

After dinner with some big donors, I take off my tie and dress shirt and lie back on my hotel bed to call Reagan.

"Hi," she says.

"Hey, babe. How was your flight?"

"Good. How was the rally?"

"Crowded." I stand up to get a bottle of water from the mini fridge. "Did you watch the press conference?"

"I did. I'm so happy for you, Jude."

"For us."

She sighs softly into the phone. I get that skin-prickling sense that something is wrong again.

"Everything okay?" I ask.

"Yeah…I wish we weren't back to cryptic conversations, though."

I unscrew the cap from my water and take a long sip. "Babe, if there's something you need to say to me, say it. I'm not worried about anything between us being used against me, and if it is, I'll handle it."

After a long pause, she says, "At the airport earlier, it was hard for me to leave you."

"It was hard for me too. We don't have to be apart, Ray. Come be with me. I want you here."

"It would look like I only came back because of the news conference."

"Since when do we give a shit what things look like? You and me, that's all that matters."

"I know, I just…I don't know, Jude."

"Whatever it is, just say it. I know you've had something on your mind, and it's driving me fucking nuts that you won't tell me what."

My heart pounds harder as I wait for her to speak. We

don't keep secrets from each other, and it makes me uneasy that she's been holding out on me.

"My mom and I have been talking a lot," she finally says. "And she…she doesn't want this life for me."

"What life?"

"The life of a politician's wife."

I rub my eyes, which are aching with fatigue from the long day. "But you married a politician five years ago. Why does she suddenly feel this way?"

"I think she just didn't want to say anything. And the governor's race has shone a brighter spotlight on us than before."

I sit on the edge of the bed, leaning my elbows on my knees. "I get why she feels that way, after what happened to her. But how do *you* feel?"

"I feel…" She pauses, seeming to think about it. "Like finding myself with no job and no job offer was the best thing that could have happened to me. I've had a lot of quiet time down here. Time to think and relax and just… be. It's made me realize how long I've been running in circles, never feeling like I'm doing enough."

"I can understand that. Babe, if you want to take time away from working, or never go back at all, I'm good with that. I just want you to be happy."

She sighs softly, making me think of last night. God, the sound of her heavy breathing as she tried not to make a sound drove me wild.

"I know. All this stuff with my mom has made me realize that life goes at the same speed whether you're taking time to appreciate the small things or not."

Her hidden messages are making me nervous. I stand up and pace over to the window in my room.

"Babe, what do you want? You don't need to explain why or anything, just tell me, bottom line—what do you want?"

"I want a quieter life. With you. I want to take vacations and shop for groceries together and watch football games every weekend during the season. I want to have babies, and I want us to raise them together. I want you to walk in the door every evening and go to bed with me every night."

I'm taken aback. For a few seconds, I can't think of anything to say. This is so unlike my driven, ambitious wife.

"Why didn't you say anything last night?" I ask her. "We could've talked about this.

There's a smile in her voice as she says, "We were kind of focused on other stuff."

"You should've said something. Why do I feel like you were scared to tell me all this?"

She exhales deeply. "Because what I want, I can't have."

"Why not?"

"Jude." Her voice is edged with irritation. "You know

why. If you win this race, you'll be working your ass off every day. We'll have security details. It's the opposite of what I'm talking about. I want you to stop being everyone's champion and just be…mine."

I nod, even though she can't see me. I can't get over my shock at what she's saying. I've been asking her to start a family with me for three years now, and she's finally saying she wants to. But she's right—as governor, I can't give her the simple life she wants.

"I need some time to think about things," I say, quickly adding, "but I don't mean us. I mean the rest of it. I love you and plan to be with you until I'm an old, grouchy bastard."

She laughs softly. "I'm not asking you to drop out of the race, baby. You've worked too hard for it. I'm just telling you why I need to be here right now. I just have to resign myself to what I have instead of what I wish I had."

*What I wish I had.* Her words are like a knife to my chest. When I promised that her happiness would be my life's goal on our wedding day, I meant it. And the thing she wants is so easy—more of me. More of us.

But she's right. I won't make empty promises about date nights and vacations after the election. Being the governor is a demanding job. I'll always make time for her, but not the way she's telling me she wants.

I won't be able to make myself unrecognizable in a

crowd. I can't say I'll walk in the door at dinnertime every evening.

"Let me think on things, okay?" I say.

"Okay. But, Jude—I think it's me who needs to do the thinking."

"What do you mean?" My blood pumps hot and fast. "Don't say you're thinking about not being with me, because that's not an option."

"I don't know what I'm thinking about, honestly. I'm still processing all of this."

I sigh heavily. "Your timing couldn't be worse. I'm two weeks out from the election, in a dead heat, and now I have to wonder if my wife's leaving me or not."

"Jude."

"Reagan."

"I'm not going anywhere right now, okay?"

I scowl. "I feel so much better, thanks."

"Let's sleep on things and talk tomorrow."

I mutter a goodnight and hang up. She might be able to sleep tonight, but I sure as hell won't.

# 25

# REAGAN

Jude strides across the stage and shakes hands with Gloria Rush, the Democratic candidate for governor. I feel a tug in my chest. His confident smile and his polished, dark suit with a red tie remind me of days gone by.

I just watched his final pre-election debate on my laptop. I'm sitting on the bed in my mom's guest room, legs crossed, wearing a gray tank top and jean shorts.

I should be wearing something much nicer right now. I should be backstage at the debate, about to hug my husband and congratulate him on crushing that debate.

He was strong but compassionate; optimistic but realistic. The debate showcased all his best qualities.

I noticed the fatigue on his face, though. The slight purple circles under his eyes that aren't usually there. And my stomach dropped with guilt from knowing it was my fault.

The broadcast switches to analysts doing post-debate coverage, and I close the cover to my laptop, grab my phone, and send Jude a text.

**You were amazing, baby. I'm so proud of you.**

My pride in him is only matched by my disappointment in myself. I've been thinking nonstop about things, and I've found some clarity that makes me wish I never would have told Jude what I did.

I put him in an impossible situation. Made him feel like he has to choose his career or our marriage, and he's right —I did it at the worst possible time.

Never did I expect to find myself out of a job. That, and my mom's unexpected cancer scare, left me feeling unmoored for the second time in my life.

The first time was after learning about my father's affair and secret family. That bombshell made me realize I wasn't pursuing a career in politics for myself, but for my father. And in an instant, he became someone I no longer cared about impressing. I realized who he was to me—a hero who sacrificed time with his family to make others' lives better—was just a façade.

I'd been working behind the scenes in politics since, and it wasn't until Andrea Matisse offered me a job that I even considered doing anything else.

I walked into my mom's kitchen and opened the freezer, going right for the Cherry Garcia. Sitting down on a counter barstool, I opened it and mined a good first bite while considering my situation.

What do I have if I no longer have my career? Who am I if I'm not a tenacious, can-do advocate for bipartisanship.

I'm Reagan Titan. Wife. Daughter. Sister. Friend. Hopefully one day, mother. I love the beach. I make amazing chocolate chip cookies. I never tire of cheesy 90s movies. I'm kind of a whiz at trivia. I'm a champion for women's rights. And I'm wound inextricably with the man who is my best friend, lover, and life partner.

I don't know where the next chapter of my life will take me. But I know Jude will be in that chapter, as he will be in every chapter after.

Do I yearn to be a governor's wife? Not especially. But I'm deeply in love with a man who stands a great chance of becoming a governor in twelve days.

My mom comes into the kitchen, her hair wrapped in a towel and a white bathrobe secured around her waist. She grabs a spoon from a kitchen drawer and sits down next to me, silently sharing my ice cream. We're getting close to the bottom before I finally speak.

· "It's hard for me not to know what direction I want to go," I say softly.

"Focus on what you *do* know."

"I love Jude. I want to be there for him—whatever that means. He stands in Sephora with me for as long as it takes me to pick out what I want, and he never complains. He rubs my back and lets me be irrational when I have PMS. He's my person, you know?" My voice breaks with emotion on the last part.

"You're his person too."

"I should've been there tonight. I let him down, and I didn't even have a good reason."

She puts an arm around me. "I shouldn't have said what I did to you. It doesn't matter what life I want for you—it matters what life you want for yourself."

"I want *him*. I wish we could have more time together than we do, and a simpler life, but Jude…he needs to do this work. He does it for veterans and people who need jobs. And he's good at it. He listens to people and then does his best to make decisions that are best for everyone. He's honest."

"We need more like him."

I look down at the empty ice cream container. "I need to go be with my husband. I owe him twelve days of the hardest campaigning I've ever done."

"I owe you an apology, Reagan. Jude is not like your father. Your life with him is not the same as my life with your father. I want you two to make your own decisions, and it warms my heart to see how much you love each other."

"Thanks, Mom."

She hugs me close. "Better go book that flight."

I nod and head to the bedroom to do just that. I hope Jude can forgive his normally decisive, headstrong wife for being flaky and unsupportive these last few days.

# 26

# JUDE

My campaign bus smells like coffee and unshowered bodies. It's been rank for the past few days as we all bust our asses heading into the homestretch.

"We're still within the margin of error," Tyson reminds us, dampening the interns' celebration of our post-debate bump in polls.

I'm leading by a hair now, but like Tyson said, it's still anyone's game.

I want this win so bad I can taste it. Gloria Rush doesn't support increased funding for veterans' assistance, which is desperately needed. The vets of Illinois will be measurably better off with me as governor. I don't want them having to fight for what they've earned, and I don't want them feeling ashamed of asking for what they need.

A story in a Chicago paper this morning about a

murder-suicide by a vet with PTSD hit me hard. If he'd gotten treatment, that tragedy could have been prevented.

"We stay on message," Tyson tells the group. "And we review the message with every new group of volunteers knocking on doors. *Every time, guys.* Message is everything right now."

The door to the bus opens, and I look over at Rita, who's smiling at whoever she opened it for. I furrow my brow in confusion, because my entire core team is on this bus right now.

"Did someone order pizza?" an intern asks hopefully.

As the person steps up onto the bus, my breath catches in my throat. It's Reagan, her dark hair back in a ponytail. She's wearing a tank top and sweats, her arms wrapped around herself.

"Babe, I didn't know you were coming." I stand up and walk to the front of the bus to greet her, rubbing her chilly upper arms.

She gives me a smile that makes me suddenly feel soft inside.

"I wanted to surprise you. Could you use another volunteer?"

There's an apology in her tone. I nod and pull her against my chest, hugging her tight.

"You're freezing, babe. What are you doing wearing a tank top in October?"

She laughs against me. "I know. I planned on going

home for clothes first, but…I was too excited to see you, and I came straight here."

"I'm glad you did."

"I'm sorry," she whispers in my ear.

I lean back and kiss her forehead, then turn to Tyson.

"Toss me that hoodie. We're gonna go grab coffee."

Several of the interns' eyes gleam at the mention of coffee. It's how we're surviving these days.

"I'll bring back coffee for anyone who wants it. Somebody text me a group order for Starbucks."

Tyson tosses me the black hoodie I sometimes wear when the bus is cold, and I help Reagan into it. The sleeves hang past her hands and the bottom comes to her thighs, but it'll keep her warm.

"I'll take door-knocking today if you need me," she says to Tyson.

Tyson looks down at his clipboard. "I need…door-knockers and mailer-stuffers."

"I'm up for anything," Reagan says.

I take her hand and lead her off of the bus. As soon as we're alone, I wrap her up in another hug and then kiss her.

"Why didn't you tell me you were coming?" I ask. "I might've actually slept last night if I'd known."

"I'm sorry." She shakes her head, her blue eyes glistening. "I've been a shitty wife lately."

"Don't say that. Never say that. You told me what was on your mind, and there's nothing wrong with that."

"Well…I've just been thrown off-balance by losing my job."

"Which wouldn't have happened if I wasn't running for governor. It's not your fault."

She sighs softly. "I know. I've just had lots of time at my mom's to think about what matters most to me. And it's not a job or an elected office or money. It's you. My family."

I nod. "I've been thinking too, and you're right. I don't want all our memories of this time in our life to be about campaigning and rallies and fancy dinners. I want a family with you. And if you're ready… I mean, if you want me to… I'll walk away from this."

"Jude, you can't."

"I can."

"This is your dream. I don't want you giving up your dream for me."

I shake my head. "For *us*, babe. And this isn't my dream—you are."

Tears well in her eyes. "Wow. You never stop amazing me, Jude. But honestly, no—I don't want you to drop out. I don't know for sure what the future holds for us, but I know how many times you've put me first, and it's my turn to put you first. Just promise you'll keep me by your side if you win."

"You aren't sure about that? Reagan, I always want you by my side."

"I know, but there'll be special interests and pressure, and—"

"Always. You're first, and everyone else is second. That's never gonna change."

She nods and smiles. "I think you're gonna do this, Jude. I was looking over the poll numbers on the flight, and I have a feeling it'll be you."

I kiss her forehead again. "We have to keep campaigning like we're behind, though."

"I know. And I'm all in. Anything you need. However I can help. I want to make up for the time I missed here."

I wink at her. "You can make that up to me between the sheets, babe."

Her sweet, sexy laugh makes my cock stir to life. "Like I said, I'm at your service."

"Excellent."

I zip up the hoodie and take her hand, heading toward the Starbucks I saw on the way to our parking spot.

"How'd you find us?" I ask, giving her a puzzled look as we walk.

"Tyson."

"Ah. You guys are becoming BBFs on me, aren't you?"

"I wouldn't go that far. But we are having friendship bracelets made."

Her quick wit was one of the first things I fell in love with. I squeeze her hand, using the other one to wave at the driver of a car who honks at us and waves, yelling, "I'm voting for you!" out his open car window.

"Thanks, man!" I wave back at him.

We make it to the coffee shop, which has a line. I look at Reagan as we wait.

"I was thinking that, win or lose, we should take a trip after the election," I say.

She considers. "Yeah, but…if it's win, there'll be tons of transition work to start on."

"It'll wait."

"Is there somewhere you want to go?"

I shrug. "Somewhere private with a beach. That's all I care about."

"That sounds nice."

When we get to the front of the line, I take out my phone to look at the coffee order and end up ordering fourteen drinks. A couple waiting for their order asks me to take a photo with them, and Reagan takes one for them.

Each carrying two trays of drinks, we start the walk back to the bus.

"If we win, I want you to know this job isn't gonna take me over," I tell her. "You know how cranky I get when I don't get to be with you for even a couple days. We get to make our own rules for this."

She nods, her expression softening with a smile. "I like

that plan. And if you win, I'd like to focus on advocacy. I don't think I want to get another job right now." She laughs. "Can you believe I just said that?"

"I think that sounds perfect. You can travel with me. What kind of advocacy do you want to do?"

"I'm not sure yet. Something with women's rights, probably. That may not thrill some of your donors."

"Makes no difference at all. I'll be proud of you for doing what matters to you."

The bus comes into sight, and the closer we get, the more it sets in that we won't have many moments like this until that post-election vacation. When it's just me and her, we'll be too exhausted for much besides sleep.

Well, *she* will. I can always manage the energy for sex with my wife.

"Babe," I say, stopping outside the open bus doors. "We can just do one term if you want, okay?"

She smiles and nods. "We make the rules."

I kiss her before walking back onto the bus. Finally, everything's right. I care more about having Reagan at my side than I do about winning or losing.

But I'm gonna do my damnedest to win.

# 27

# REAGAN

Jude grabs a glass of champagne from a passing server's tray and passes it to me.

"Drink," he says with a wink.

I sip it gratefully, feeling more like throwing back the entire glass at once.

God, I'm nervous. The polls were running so close yesterday that we still don't know who's likely to win. Considering how recently I wasn't sure I wanted my husband to be governor, it's ironic that I'm now hoping for it with everything I've got.

And worse, I can't let it show that I'm a bundle of nerves. We cleaned up and left headquarters to come to an evening election-night party put on by wealthy supporters.

It's nice seeing the aides and interns from the campaign

all cleaned up, the men showered and shaved and the women wearing makeup and fancy gowns.

I'm pretty sure that like me, they'd prefer to be scarfing down pizza from a box right now as we all hover in front of the TV making inappropriate jokes and waiting for returns to come in—but they deserve to be here. They're taking advantage of the open bar, but Jude and I decided to stay sober.

Looks like he changed his mind about me drinking, though. I think it was a good call, because I'm about to jump out of my skin.

I'm staring at a TV monitor set up for us to watch the returns come in, and Jude takes my hand and tugs gently.

"Let's mingle, babe. Somebody'll let us know when it gets updated."

I blow out a nervous breath. "Okay."

He slides an arm around my waist, and we walk over to a group of couples. Everyone shakes Jude's hand and asks him what his first order of business is going to be.

"Win or lose, we're taking a vacation," he tells them. "We're leaving Friday morning."

"You certainly deserve it," one of the women says. "This has been a hard-fought race."

One of the men, who I'm pretty sure is one of the Branch brothers, rolls his eyes. "That happens when you're fighting a millionaire willing to spend whatever it takes."

Jude was outspent almost three-to-one by Gloria Rush.

His supporters came through with a lot of money, but she spent a record amount for a gubernatorial race.

I'm incredibly proud of Jude, no matter what happens. He took the high road at every turn, and he worked his ass off.

We agreed this morning after the quickest quickie we've ever had that we have no regrets. Whether it's from the governor's mansion or our home in Chicago, we know life has good times in store for us.

Tyson approaches us, grinning. "Cook County came in. You're still up enough that a recount's off the table."

Jude lets out a breath and pulls me close, kissing the top of my head. Then he rests a palm on my back, exposed by the low-back red sequined gown I'm wearing.

The moment he saw me walk out of the bathroom of our hotel room in this dress, he told me he couldn't wait to get it off me.

People come up to Jude to offer congratulations, some taking selfies with him. I can read his expression—he's not ready to celebrate until Tyson tells him he's been called as the projected winner.

I pass Jude my champagne glass, and he takes a swig, wrinkling his nose.

"Too sweet."

Tyson looks down at his phone screen and then back up at Jude.

"CNN's projecting it." He breaks into a grin. "Congratulations, Governor."

Jude embraces Tyson in a back-patting man hug. I can't help the tears that fall to my cheeks. It's not just because Jude won, but because I know what he's been through to get here.

My husband's road to the governor's mansion started in the Middle East, where he served with pride and resolved to help his fellow veterans. A woman who lost part of her leg in service came up to him outside our polling place this morning and shook his hand, tearfully wishing him well.

When he sweeps me into his arms and holds me tight, my feet leave the floor.

"We did it," he says, his voice quaking with emotion as he buries his face in my shoulder.

"I love you." I put my hands on his cheeks and kiss away the moisture on his cheek. "Congratulations, babe."

He sets me down and takes a deep breath, steadying himself. "Should I call Gloria?"

"No, *she'll* call *you*, remember?"

He grins sheepishly. "Right. I can't even think straight right now. I can't believe this."

"Believe it, love. You have your speech, right?"

He pats the breast pocket of his suit. "Yeah. I want you up there with me."

"I will be." I finish the champagne and smile at him.

"Probably a good time to call all the aides and interns together and thank them."

"Right. I think Tyson got a room for us to meet in for that."

Texts of congratulations start hitting my phone from family, friends, and colleagues. My mouth drops open in surprise when I see one come in from Andrea Matisse.

**Andrea: Congratulations to your husband. Would love to discuss my job opportunity with you again.**

Ha. I'm not even going to respond to her. Anyone who didn't stand by us when the chips were down doesn't deserve loyalty.

Besides, I don't want to be a globe-trotter for Andrea's foundation. As first lady of my state, I can choose my own advocacy projects.

If anyone had told me when I was in my early twenties that this daughter of a Democratic senator, who served as a Democratic state rep, would end up being the wife of a Republican governor and not wanting to hold a full-time job, I would have laughed hysterically.

Me? In love with a man of the opposing political party? Not blazing trails with an exhausting travel schedule, but wanting to be by my husband's side instead?

Impossible, I would have thought.

But that's the thing about women's rights—I support women choosing their own path, free from judgment.

Stay-at-home mom, First Lady, physicist, mechanic—

they're all my people, and I hope to bring *all* women's issues into the spotlight.

I stand in the back of the room as Jude addresses the group of people who worked on his campaign. Many of them are crying as he thanks them for their tireless work. Gratitude overwhelms me, and I'm near tears, too.

Tyson approaches and leans against the wall next to me.

"Congratulations," I say, offering him my hand.

His handshake is weak, but his smile is broad. "Thanks. You too."

"You're coming to work for him now, right?"

He shrugs. "I will if he asks."

"He'll ask."

Tyson's smile fades. "I thought you might not want that."

"I can't think of anyone better. You've done a fantastic job. I mean, chief of staff's a grind, but if you want it—"

"I do."

I punch him playfully in the shoulder. "I'll put in a good word."

"Thanks, boss."

"Seriously, Tyson, you came through in every way. I'm not sure he would have made it without you."

Tyson's cheeks redden. "Thanks." After an awkward silence, he lowers his brows and says, "Are we gonna be friends now?"

I shrug. "I'm kinda used to our dynamic."

"Me too."

"Let's keep 'em guessing."

We share a brief laugh and then both focus on Jude.

"Reagan and I consider you more family than friends," he says, his voice catching in his throat. "Thanks doesn't seem like enough to say for all the months you guys devoted to the campaign. I'll just say…" He clears his throat. "I promise I'll do my best to make you proud."

The interns in the front row start cheering, jumping up from their chairs and throwing their arms in the air. Jude's gaze wanders across the crowd, and I know he's looking for me.

I head for the front of the room, and as soon as Jude spots me, he opens his arms, wrapping one around me when I reach him.

"How 'bout an Al/Tipper kiss?" he asks in a low tone.

I laugh at his reference to the infamous, lengthy kiss from the 2000 presidential campaign, then nod. We're not in front of the cameras here—it's just our supporters.

He dips me like we're dancing and then plants a long, deep kiss on my mouth, making everyone in the room hoot and holler.

When we stand up, he can't seem to stop smiling at me. And I'm feeling the same way.

I never dreamed we'd end up here, but now, I can't imagine being anywhere else.

# 28

# JUDE

THE SUNRISE WAKES ME UP, LIGHT STREAMING THROUGH the tiny cracks in our primitive beach hut.

I glance over at Reagan, who looks like an angel as she sleeps soundly, curled up on one side with her dark hair around her shoulders.

Brushing a stray lock away from her face, I study her. I don't just see beauty. There's grace. Strength. Humor. Compassion.

Somehow, I'm lucky enough to be living the life of my dreams. If and when we have children, I'll have all I've ever wanted.

Reagan is right—we can't let our marriage get lost in the mix. I'm going to show her I meant what I said about prioritizing us.

And if I'm a one-term governor, I'll be good with it. I don't want to go any further in politics than this. In fact, I didn't even want to go this far, but the party leadership begged me due to a lack of other decent candidates.

When Reagan stirs, I slip my arm around her waist. A smile touches her lips, and she opens her eyes.

"Hey," she says in a sleepy tone. "Good morning."

"Morning, babe." I kiss her lips lightly.

"No, I have morning breath."

"For the eleven hundredth time, I don't care."

She cringes. "I care."

I kiss her harder and she tries to shrink away, but I hold her in place.

"What are we doing today?" she asks, yawning.

Our beach hut is right in the crystal-clear water, with a wooden walkway to the beach in back and stairs into the water in front.

Yesterday was our first day here, and we spent it walking on the beach, swimming, and fucking our brains out. It was perfection.

"Want to go eat at that restaurant we heard about later?" I suggest.

"Yeah, let's do dinner there."

"And I'm thinking we can spend the rest of the day right here. Maybe take an occasional break to swim?"

She laughs and cups my cheek in her hand. "Babe, you're insatiable."

"Guilty."

She reaches between my legs and palms my half-hard cock. I close my eyes and soak in the sensation of her stroking me.

So fucking good.

There's no such thing as politics in this little hut. Just me and my dead sexy wife, spending the next ten days focused entirely on each other.

She kisses my chest and slides onto her knees, working her way down. I stretch out and groan as she gets to my cock, her hot breath on the tip a tease of what's to come.

Her tongue toys with my head, circling and stroking until I don't think I can take anymore. Then she sinks down and takes me as deep as she can, and I slide my hand into her hair, her name coming out of my mouth in a ragged tone.

We've been together so long that she knows exactly how to drive me wild. She reads my signals perfectly.

A buddy asked me before I got married if I was sure I only wanted one woman's mouth on my dick for the rest of my life, and I told him that, without a doubt, I was.

Reagan doesn't just give me head. Cheesy as it sounds, I feel like she's loving my body at moments like this. Making my pleasure her only goal, just as I make hers mine.

I'll never want another woman like this, and I'll never love another woman like this. I hope Reagan and I get to be old and gray together, but if not, no other woman could ever take her place.

I could love again, sure, but not like this. It wouldn't be love that seared me and lifted me at the same time. Reagan and I are two halves that make a whole.

She moves down to my balls, making me groan hard and fist the bedsheet. This is how she drives me to the brink.

Slowly. Carefully. Perfectly.

I'm breathing hard when she finally returns to my cock, her lips and tongue ravishing every nerve ending. My grunts and groans are running together as I race toward the point of no return.

When she looks up at me, her milk-chocolate eyes full of love, longing, and mischief as she sinks her mouth down onto my length, I come with a mighty roar.

Fuck, it's good. I'm gonna make sure she has an orgasm that matches that one before we leave this hut.

After we clean up, we snuggle back under the sheet together, the muggy temperature already coating us both in a layer of sweat.

I kiss my wife, and she starts to doze back off to sleep. I'll lie here and hold her until she wakes up.

I can't wait for our future together. But I also vow to live our present to the fullest, because really, that's what matters most.

Not then. Not the maybes. Not the what-ifs. Not tomorrow.

Now. And our now is everything I've ever wanted.

241

# ABOUT BRENDA ROTHERT

Brenda Rothert is an Illinois native who was a print journalist for nine years. She made the jump from fact to fiction in 2013 and never looked back. From new adult to steamy contemporary romance, Brenda creates fresh characters in every story she tells. She's a lover of Diet Coke, chocolate, lazy weekends and happily ever afters.

Subscribe to Brenda's newsletter:
brendarothert.com/subscribe

Learn more about Brenda's books:
http://brendarothert.com/

Click here to learn more about the Chicago Blaze series!

Chelle's a full-time writer, time-waster extraordinaire, social media addict, coffee fiend, and ex-history teacher.

To learn more about Chelle's books, please visit menofinked.com.

*Ready for more hot & sexy alphas?*

**Join my newsletter** by visiting
*menofinked.com/news*

**Get New Release Text Notifications (US only)**
➔ Text **BLISS** to **24587**

Join my **Private Facebook Reader Group** at
*facebook.com/groups/blisshangout*

*Want to drop me a line?*
menofinked.com/contact

**Where to Follow Me:**

www.ingramcontent.com/pod-product-compliance
Lightning Source LLC
Chambersburg PA
CBHW061433150726
47987CB00001B/193